*Alaska's Aleutian Islands Series*
*Book 1*

# RESCUED

## TRUDY
## SAMSILL

## Acknowledgments

- *To Almighty God, who has given me life and the passion to write. May my passion bring You fame.*

- *To my husband and greatest fan. Your love for Alaska and God's people inspired this series. I'm so grateful for you and your belief in me and in us. And as you said, "God's not through writing our redemption story." I look forward to what is in store for our future.*

- *To my wonderful children. All of your sweet notes of encouragement, the cups of coffee you brought to me, the hugs and neck rubs after a long day of writing, these all have given me just another push in the direction I desired to go. And what would I have done without my teenage son, Bryse, who helped me with my e-book cover and formatting and other technicalities of the book? You bless me!*

- *To my mother, Jane, and sister, Amy, my loudest "cheerleaders." As I have said before, if I wrote the simple words "The dog ran down the street" you would both cheer loudly for me! You have read and re-read every word and change in this book and kept asking for me to hurry up and finish the next chapter so you could see what happened next. You have kept the wheels rolling on this project!*

- *To my friend and challenger, Jana, the one that asked questions and pushed me to improve the details and story. I won't forget the day you said to me after reading the first few chapters, "It feels like you took my plate away from me and I wasn't through eating!" Thank you for this nudge to press on and finish!*

- *To Emma. You jumped in on this project towards the end and used your writer's "eagle eye." You spotted things that I would have never seen. Thank you!! I look forward to having you on future projects!*

*PSALM 136:23-24*
*(CEV)*

*God saw the trouble we were in.*

*God's love never fails.*

*He rescued us from our enemies.*

*God's love never fails.*

# CHAPTER 1

*February, 1968*

Gabe awoke with a start. Glancing out his bedroom window of his family's Little River, Washington home, the moon's height told him he hadn't been asleep long. Several nights in a row that same dream brought him from sound sleep to wide awake, leaving him with the recurring feeling of almost being able to grasp something just out of his reach. Gabe ran his hands through his short sandy hair. He stretched his six foot frame out on the bed and tried to relax. Dreams were not a common occurrence for Gabe. Usually he had no trouble resting and enjoying uninterrupted sleep. But not this week.

*A girl's hand with long, slender, light-brown fingers reached out towards him. Straight, glossy black hair trailed behind an unseen face. The girl was running, giggling, urging him to follow her. Her laughter and out-stretched hand beckoned Gabe. He could see his own hand reaching for hers, reaching, trying to grasp her hand, but not able to touch her. Her giggles continued, then were suddenly cut short by a sharp, loud crack, like the sound of a gun, then the blood-curdling scream. Gabe tried to grab the hand but missed as he saw the faceless girl tumble down a black abyss, screaming, her hand still grasping for his....*

*********************

In the early pre-dawn hours of the Alaskan morning, Rose lay in her bed savoring the aftermath of the dream, her secret dream. Something she didn't even tell her best friend, Luka. Snuggling down in her bed of furs, Rose tried to fight off the early morning chill and warm up her icy nose again. One of the hardest parts in her day was to coax her tired body from the comforting warmth of bed and re-enter the frigid temperatures of the day. Bedtime was her time. No responsibilities, no icy hands and feet, no constant mental check-list of the daily routine to make life bearable on the Aleutian Islands.

These were the hard months of life here on the Islands. The monotony and drudgery of the day-to-day work just to survive weighed on the Aleutian Indians. Survival was the way of life.

Thus Rose's escape truly took place at bedtime under her piles of furs. With the sounds of her parents' light breathing and her older brother's snoring drifting in and out of her still sleepy mind, Rose allowed herself to remember her dream, full of colors she was unaccustomed to.

*Shades of blue, some bright, some deeper, hovered in front of her eyes. Slowly she could make out brilliant blue eyes set in a tanned face with a halo of golden hair. The face's features were unclear, but the blue eyes were unmistakable. Strong, bronzed hands held toys out to her, toys she had seen before but couldn't name. Toys, not of her world, but ones she had touched, stark reminders of the difference in this angel-man's world of gold, blue, red and green and her world of browns, whites, grays, and duller hues. His dark blue legs walked towards her, encouraging Rose to see what he was holding, to play with the strange beautiful items. She smiled up into his blue eyes and reached for a toy, but instead, noticed a book tucked under his strong arm. Instead of the pretty red object, she reached to touch the black book he held.....*

# CHAPTER 2

Randall and Rebecca Parker sat across from each other at the family's breakfast table. The view to their right just past the kitchen window was stunning. The snow-topped mountains of Washington were their "backyard." Several deer were quietly having their breakfast in the Parkers' backyard during the morning's quiet hours at sunrise. Randall and Rebecca were sipping coffee together and enjoying each others' company.

Becca looked up from her morning devotional book. "Rand, I've been thinking. We need to decide if we are going to continue to return to the Aleutian Indians or if God wants us to turn our mission field over to another couple. You know we will both be 50 in a few weeks. Are we getting too old for this kind of work?"

Rand looked at his sweet Becca. "Fifty? No way! We just finished college, got married, and began missions work with the Aleutian Indians a couple of years ago, didn't we? Don't rush us into the 'too old' phase just yet." Randall paused, seeing Becca's sincerity. "Seriously, honey, my concern is not for us. I believe we still have many more years of missions work left in us. Unless you are having reservations? You love the Aleutian people as much as I do.

What's really behind you questioning something that we are both so very passionate about? This has been our life's work outside of teaching school."

Rand took Becca's small hand in his. In a flash, he could see her precious hands and the many ways she used them to hug, teach, comfort, and give to those needy in Alaska. The little ones loved to hold her hand and walk with her. The young pre-teen girls would copy the deft movements of Becca's hands as she taught them to make bread. And the dear old Indians relaxed at the touch of Becca's cool hand on their fevered, wrinkled brow. To Rand, her hands were an extension of her heart, always reaching out, always giving comfort, always helping the needy. Yet, somehow his Becca made sure Rand was her number one priority, and he knew it. God had truly blessed him.

Rebecca took her time to respond. "I don't know what's wrong with me. Maybe it's just turning fifty that has me questioning my life and what it should look like at this stage. Missions work at fifty? Should we still continue to do it? I do love the Aleutians, but I just don't want my desires to overshadow what is best for them. Would a younger couple better suit their needs? What do you think?"

Rand laughed softly. "Becca, when I look at you I still see the young girl I married years ago, the one that chose to share the same Alaskan adventure that was in my heart, the young girl that said 'Yes!' to whatever God had planned for us to do. And I still see that same woman now. Don't question 'why' we should continue to do something just because you think it is what we *should* ask at fifty. Let the question be 'why not?'"

Rand looked deeply into eyes he had adored for many years, to the places of her heart that only he knew, knowing they did share one concern in common. "I am more concerned about Gabe. He's the one on the threshold of change, not us almost-fifty-year-olds. Gabe is 21, just finished getting his associate's degree and not sure what to do with himself. Are we holding him back from pursuing a career, making him feel like he *has* to continue to help his aging parents on the mission field? Or does he know he is free to do whatever God wants him to do? Of course, we can use him and benefit from the knowledge he gained and his college degree, but what does God want? What does Gabe want? That's my concern."

Becca flipped open her Bible next to her plate of unfinished cinnamon toast. "I just read this morning Proverbs 16:9 and 19:21. Both apply to Gabriel and his future. Let me read them to you, honey." She quickly flipped to the passage and read to Rand. "'A man's heart plans his way, but the

LORD directs his steps.' The other verse says, 'There are many plans in a man's heart, nevertheless the LORD's counsel — that will stand.'"

She paused for a moment reflecting on what she had just read. "Randall, God is wanting us to trust Him to direct our son and that He will steer him in the right direction, regardless of what Gabe *thinks* he should do with his future. God's plan and purpose for Gabe will stand. We have to believe that. A person can plan all day what they want to do with their life and head in a certain direction for a while, but I think there will always be that nagging, that pulling in the direction God wants them to go. If Gabe has a heart to do what God wills, which we both know he does, then God will direct Gabe and his future."

Rand's eyes quickly misted over at the beauty and grace and well-timed words from God through his wife. Until now, he hadn't realized just how worried he was about Gabe. Randall leaned over and kissed Becca on the cheek. "Finish your toast, honey. I think I will go for a walk in the woods and talk to God about this. Prayer is a must when decisions have to be made. Thanks for the verses. I agree; we trust God with Gabe."

Leaving through the back screened door, Randall headed down the well-worn path into the woods, the place where most of his life decisions and problems were hashed out between him, God, and nature.

# CHAPTER 3

Edward Hamilton, Gabe's best friend and occasional Alaska mission trip companion, drove up the Parker's tree-lined driveway. Ed always seemed to know when it was close to dinner-time at the Parker's. Like another son to them, Rand and Becca always had extra to feed Ed when he arrived.

Ed picked a good night to show up for dinner. Rand was grilling steaks over their backyard fire pit that could rival any steakhouse around. Becca was making her special scalloped potatoes, a fresh salad, and homemade rolls. He knew there would be a wonderful dessert and coffee to follow dinner.

Rand greeted Ed and invited him to the fire pit while he cooked the steaks. Easing his long legs ending in cowboy boots up onto the end of a lounge chair, Ed drank in the cool, early-evening temperature, the smell of cedar trees, and cooking meat.

Ed had never lost his Texan, gentlemanly charm, nor had he given up his favorite attire, Wrangler jeans, boots, and a t-shirt that was usually topped with a pearl-snap denim shirt. At six feet, two inches, dark brown hair, and crystal blue eyes, Ed's looks easily caught the ladies' eyes. Ed was a people person. Everyone that knew him was drawn to his warm, friendly personality, his slow Texan drawl, and his peaceful, non-rushed demeanor. He grinned his half-grin at Rand and began to relax for the first time that day, the reality sinking in as it always did when he was at the Parkers'.

Born and raised in Texas until he was a freshman in high school, Ed and his parents moved to Washington when he was fourteen. Both his parents were alcoholics. Ed was raised around booze, all night parties, and learning at an early age to fend for himself. Not four years ago, Ed would have been found in some bar drinking the night away along with his depression.

His literal run-in with Gabriel had saved his life. Stumbling out of a bar one evening, he rounded a corner and collided with Gabe. Ed fell to the ground and would have spent the night there if not for Gabe's insistence that he get up and go with him for a cup of coffee as a means to apologize for the run-in.

Gabe knew Ed from high school. He had heard rumors of Ed's family and the parties they hosted. Gabe always felt sorry for Ed, almost guilty at times, knowing the kind of family life he had. Quickly seizing this God-ordained opportunity, Gabe coaxed cup after cup of coffee down his drunken companion, and by 6 a.m., Ed had heard for the first time about God and His great love, about how God gave His son to die for the world's sins, including Ed's, and how God wanted to set Ed free from alcohol and depression and make him into a new man. In Ed's moment of desperation he listened and decided to give God a chance and accepted Gabe's offer of friendship and help. He gave his heart and life to God, never regretting these decisions. Life had made a complete turnaround ever since that night.

Needless to say, each and every time Ed came to the Parker's home, he was aware of the gift of a second chance he had been given. Ed resolved to never take this gift or this family for granted.

Randall brought Ed out of his reverie. "You seem mighty quiet tonight, Ed. Something on your mind?"

Ed flashed his half-grin at Randall. "No, Sir. Just reflecting on how different life is now than it was a few years ago. I wouldn't be here now, smelling those great steaks if Gabe hadn't bumped into me."

Knowing the boys' story, Rand laughed at that last comment.

"Rand, I know I don't say it enough, but thank you for taking me in. And for talking me into going on that first trip to the Aleutian Islands. I needed to see there's a whole other world out there than the one I was in." Ed got up from his chair and gave Rand a big bear hug. "So when's the next trip out?"

Rand flipped the steaks and looked up to see Becca walk out with a platter. "You men look deep in conversation. Sorry to interrupt."

"No interruption, Mrs. Bee." Ed had nicknamed Becca "Mrs. Bee" because she was always buzzing around working like a bee. "I had just asked Rand when the next Aleutian trip was planned."

Becca said, "Well that seems to be the recurring topic of the day. We were just discussing that this morning. We don't know, Ed, but maybe God's wanting to replace Rand and I with someone younger. We will be fifty soon, you know. And Gabe is on the brink of decisions concerning his future. We just don't want to stop him from going the path he should because he feels like he has to continue these trips with us."

A look of shock came over Ed's face as he realized what she was implying. "Mrs. Bee, how could you say or even think such a thing? I don't mean any disrespect, but you guys are going to let a number, your age, determine your future? If you're still breathing, God's not done with you yet, unless He has spoken directly to you that He's done!"

Ed paused and took a breath before continuing. "And, Gabe, don't worry about him! Like you both tell me, God knows the plans He has for us. Do you think you can really stop Gabe from doing what God has planned for him? Gabe's listening and seeking God. He will hear."

Ed's southern upbringing and Texas charm caused him to suddenly stop talking, aware that he had never before spoken so strongly to these two beloved people. Usually he was on the listening end of things, not the lecturing end.

Becca had the look on her face as if she had just gotten a bucket of cold water thrown at her; Rand was trying to hold back a laugh and couldn't contain the smirk that kept appearing.

Ed blurted out, "Guys, I am so sorry! I shouldn't have said what I did. I'm not here to advise you on how to be parents or tell you how to run your life...."

Becca interrupted Ed with a small kiss on his cheek and a quiet, "Thank you, Ed." With that, she went back inside.

Rand finally released his held-in laugh, leaving Ed bewildered.

"What?!?! Did I just miss something?" Ed sputtered.

Rand placed a hand on Ed's shoulder. "No, Son. You just unknowingly cleared some things up for these two dense almost-fifty-year-olds."

# CHAPTER 4

Gabe squeezed in the family's driveway and parked his dad's three year-old, blue, 1965 Jeep Wagoneer. With a grin on his face he thought, *Ed always knows when it's steak night.*

He sauntered into the kitchen, savoring the aroma of his mom's homemade brownies and kissed her on the cheek. "Hey, Mom. How are you?"

She looked at her tall son. "Better. Much better."

Gabe eyed her suspiciously. "Ok....."

Becca grinned. "The guys are out back finishing the steaks. Why don't you take them a drink? There are some cans of pop in the refrigerator."

He grabbed some drinks from the refrigerator and headed through the screened back door. "Hey, guys. Need a drink?" He handed one to each of the men and collapsed in a chair close by.

Rand eyed his son. "Thanks, Gabe. How was your day? You look tired."

Gabe *was* tired. He felt tired all the way to his bones. "I spent the day chasing down job leads. Some were dead ends, some half-open doors. Why can't a job just fall in my lap while I am driving around town looking?" Gabe's usual humor was making an appearance even in the face of his frustrations. "I know God's got the right job for me. But this is harder than I thought. I've been at this for three weeks and still no possibilities. Aren't you supposed to find a job easier after you get your degree and have an abundance of leads to choose from?"

Rand looked at his son. *If only I could make this season easier for him. Job hunting is harder than it seems,* he thought. "Gabe, you keep pursuing leads, knocking on doors, and most importantly, keep trusting God."

"Thanks, Dad. It would be really easy to give up right now and just go flip burgers or deliver pizzas again, but I know you're right."

Becca stuck her head out the door and called the guys in for dinner.

It was evenings like these that Gabe really appreciated. Good food, supportive parents, and a great friend. He couldn't help compare life here in Washington, with a beautiful home at the foot of the Cascade Mountains, surrounded by blue skies, gorgeous lakes, tall trees, and beautiful wildlife to the mission experiences he'd had on the Aleutian Islands.

Life on the Aleutian Islands consisted mostly of constant fog, plenteous rain, cold temperatures, and windy days and nights. The people worked very hard, had little conveniences like in the States, and lived a much simpler life. Though he loved his life in Washington, Gabe's heart often wandered back to Alaska and its people. He always looked forward to trips to the Islands, whether it was for several weeks or several months. Since he was six years old and had literally begged his parents to go on a mission trip with them, Gabe had viewed the Aleutian Indians as a second family to him.

Unlike other kids his age, he spent his summer vacations in Alaska, playing with the Indian children even though he could barely communicate with them, while his parents brought medical supplies, held Vacation Bible Schools for the children, and worked with the adults to bring improvements to their homes or businesses. He loved the feeling of the Aleutian community and enjoyed the less complicated way of life. As Gabe grew older, his love for the people had grown as well. When he entered junior high and high school, his friends thought he was crazy for wanting to spend the summer break helping the Indians. When he entered his junior year in high school, all his friends were finally convinced that Gabe was different. He wasn't interested in dating, partying, or just hanging out. He liked to spend his time actually accomplishing something, whether it was serving soup to the homeless in his own town or helping with Vacation Bible School in Alaska.

When Gabe began his senior year in high school, the pressure was turned up by his school counselors and teachers to make a decision about college. What interested Gabe was simply how to help others, and he also was very intrigued by the geographical features of Alaska. He finally gave in and decided to attend their town's local junior college. Gabe was very efficient in organizing any event and knew how to motivate others to work to their best potential. By twenty-one, Gabe had gotten his Associate's degree in logistics hoping to get a job and then to eventually use his degree to help manage all of the ins and outs of mission trips. But now what? He couldn't seem to find a job that he could use his degree with, a degree that he felt like he would need, according to his counselors at school. This was all much more complicated than he thought it would be.

Not wanting to spoil everyone's mood at dinner with his own depressing thoughts, Gabe forced himself back to the present meal and family at hand and determined to enjoy the rest of his evening with his favorite people.

# CHAPTER 5

The pungent scent of early morning fires being stoked and fed caused Rose to stir under her fur coverings. Sleep had long ago evaded her though she hadn't yet stirred from under the warmth of her bed. Consciously, she forsook re-hashing her recurring dream knowing the day wouldn't be delayed by her staying in bed. Rose quickly dressed, adding her parka and boots before venturing out into the cold day. She was ready for a warm meal to jump-start her body and mind.

In the early stages of the Alaskan sunrise, she crunched across the frozen ground towards the stack of firewood. One of her jobs was to re-kindle the fire and get the day's first meal started. Looking around her, Rose saw the other closely placed homes coming to life. Her extended family and friends began stirring around their homes as well, beginning the day's preparation for their own.

After getting the fire going again, Rose ducked back inside and heard the sounds of her father's raspy cough. Her heart ached for him, once a strong, hard-working man. His calloused hands still bore marks of an entire life of labor. His stooped back spoke of strenuous work to provide for his family's needs. Now he only had momentary bursts of energy as most of it was spent in clearing his lungs of the deadly sickness consuming him. Her father was suffering from pneumonia. His good days were now outnumbered by the bad ones.

Many of Natalia's days were dedicated to bringing relief and comfort to her life-mate. She spoon-fed him warm soups and drinks to help with the almost constant cough on the days he couldn't leave the house. Knowing there was little else that could be done for him, Natalia gave her time to his care and comfort. She had long ago run out of the special medicine the missionaries brought to ease his worsening cough. *Will the kind missionaries return again soon? I won't have him with me much longer. I just want him to be comfortable his last days*, Natalia mused as she tucked her still-sleeping husband in under the blankets and furs.

She watched her daughter's swift, sure movements as Rose prepared their breakfast, grateful for her sweet Rose, her daughter's name a constant reminder that beauty truly can come from the midst of thorns. Rose's life was surely a testament to this fact.

Rose began heating the morning porridge and weak coffee. She knew this meager meal helped strengthen her father after his usual morning coughing fits.

On his good days, when the fits of coughing were less and he was able to get some much needed sleep, Ivan trapped animals for meat and fur or would fish. He knew his working days were numbered as each passing week his cough worsened. Sometimes a couple of weeks would go by and Ivan couldn't even leave the house. Hopefully tomorrow would be a good day, one where he could get out of bed and provide for his family and not depend on his son to do so.

Sorrow filled Ivan's heart over the future of his little family. What would happen to his precious Natalia when he was unable to work or was dead and gone? Ivan knew their son, Andrew, hated this kind of work. When Andrew turned 13, Ivan had hopes that his son would show more interest in the family trade. These last seven years had proved otherwise.

Andrew worked with Ivan, but his heart wasn't in it. Ivan continued to train his son and give him responsibilities by allowing him to have his own traps and to make a little of his own money, hoping this incentive would help get him interested. It hadn't worked. Ivan knew his only son resented the work.

He often wondered if this awful sickness he had wasn't the cause of Andrew despising the family trade because Andrew had to do much of the work alone. Necessity required son to care for ailing father, something Ivan regretted daily. He knew Andrew preferred to be in town, anywhere away from the island. Andrew had made his feelings known on more than one occasion. Would he even attempt to carry on in his father's trade or move away entirely from Datka Island to pursue his own desires?

Ivan worried mostly about Natalia. He knew she was working later and later into the night to produce more baskets and clothes to sell to provide for them. He had hoped his son would begin to help out more with the fishing and trapping on the days he couldn't work when he was sick, but lately, the only days Andrew agreed to work were when Natalia had been so worried she was reduced to tears at the lack of money or food in their house. Then Andrew would work for a few hours and return home with a meager catch before leaving again to be with his friends. His twenty year-old son was slowly drifting away from the family, away to heaven only knew what, causing Ivan to lay awake at night with deep fear and anxiety over Andrew and the future.

Ivan's only consolation was their sweet Rose and her heart to serve and work and love her family. She never resented his sickness, though it caused more work for her. Rose honored her parents like no other daughter could. Ivan knew he would die a proud man, proud of the woman she was becoming, proud he was her father.

*******************

After preparing and serving the meal Rose looked around outside at the beginnings of the day's activities. She saw her aunt and uncle's house, not far from her own. Her aunt was already sitting outside by the fireside hard at work mending a pair of Uncle James's fur boots. Aunt Aggie was an early riser, always up before most of the village had even had their scant breakfast. She was known throughout the village for her sewing abilities.

Long ago, Aggie was taught by her own mother to mend almost anything. The Aleutians didn't have a store close by to purchase goods, clothing, or food. Their belongings had to last them a very long time, each item deemed as precious and priceless and very difficult to replace. The art of making their own clothing, from shirts to parkas to boots, had been handed down from generation to generation.

The Aleutian Indians' lives drastically changed when the American missionaries began their yearly visits to the Island. They would bring much needed medicines, clothing items, food, and tools that were a great relief to most of the Indians. The majority of the Aleutians appreciated and looked forward to their missionary friends' arrival and supplies. It brought a welcome change to the monotony of their cold, frozen world.

But there were some that were not so appreciative of the visits from the missionaries. Anger and bitterness would flare up among a few of the older, more traditional Indians who were prideful enough to not want to be seen as needy. Some of the younger men in their early twenties also despised the visits. Their pride was from a different vein; they didn't want to be seen as incompetent or "less than" an American.

It was an ongoing battle between the Americans and the prideful Aleutians. The few that weren't happy about the missionaries were constantly seeking ways to subtly remind the Americans that they weren't welcome. If it weren't for the medical help and medicines that really did help their community, they would have run them off the Island for good long ago.

The American missionaries fought to not impose their culture on the Aleutians, to only show them the love of Christ and bring aid to them. They had no desire to change their Indian friends. The battle was hard-fought from both sides.

Aggie finished up her mending and went in to seek another task to complete. There was always something to be done. She gathered up her husband's and son's clothes to mend. Aggie's supply of heavy denim, flannel, and wool material was running low. She used these supplies to make warm clothes for her family and to also help bring in an income by selling clothing to vendors at Seal Harbor on the mainland.

Quickly her thoughts turned to her only son, Joshua. The same age as Rose's 20-year-old brother, Andrew, her boy turned man, would soon be seeking a wife and starting a family of his own. Aggie's brow creased as she thought of her son.

As a child he had been strong-willed and independent, always fighting for his own way of doing things. Though a pleasant baby and little boy, when Joshua reached his early teen years, he began spending time with Peter, a new friend of his that had a bad reputation in the village. The young man was known for stealing and drinking alcohol. Peter, being two years older than Joshua and Andrew, had access to liquor that her son and nephew didn't yet have.

Peter had been raised by an alcoholic father; his mother died from pneumonia when he was only four. The boy's father refused help from everyone, making his small child spend the day with him trapping seals for their hides and meat. The father and son spent the evenings together with men that wanted to only sip from their bottles and escape the cold and pain of life. Little Peter knew of no other life but the one his father had given him.   Aggie's heart broke for the young man knowing the path he was on would only lead to destruction.

Lately, she had smelled the foul scent of alcohol on her own boy, and when she and her husband questioned him, he only lied, yelled at them for their questions, and left home for several hours in the middle of the night. She heard him creep into the house in the wee hours of the morning and crash into his bed in worse shape than before. Fear and guilt kept her quiet. She didn't want to be the reason he became angry and left the house for more. She chose to remain quiet and look the other way on the evenings her son came home reeking of alcohol. Better for him to eat something and fall in bed and pass out than for she and her husband to suffer his wrath and wonder where he was or what he was doing.

Aggie knew both husband and son would want breakfast soon and then would be heading to work, her husband working for the good of the family, her son so he could continue his habits of alcohol. James appeared first, wearing his warmest gear ready for another cold day of fishing. He fished both for their food and to have fish to sell to the Indians willing to purchase from him.

James hobbled over to his wife, his knees worn down by years of kneeling on icy ground to retrieve fish from the freezing waters. The couple loved each other dearly, even after all these many years together. Their love remained strong and true. With a quick brush of his lips on his wife's cheek, James took his breakfast, quickly ate and left for work.

Within the hour, Joshua stomped out of the house, grumbling yet again about the breakfast his mother had made and that it never changed, always the same food every day.

"Joshua, be grateful for the food we have and eat it. You need your strength to work. Your father could use any extra money you can earn for repairs on his boat. Please, Joshua, help him out. He works so hard for….."

Turning angrily at his mother's words, Joshua shouted, "I don't have any extra money for him! I work hard for my money, not to give it away to a stupid fisherman. If he was smart, when he did earn some money, Father wouldn't give it away to some poor family that can earn their own keep."

He spat on the ground and reached a hand up and fingered his mother's rainbow scarf. "Sell your useless scarf to some woman from the mainland next time you go to town. I am sure you can get a good price for an *American* item. Then give your husband the money he needs so badly."

Joshua spoke the word "American" with such venom in his voice; Aggie flinched as he flung the edge of her scarf away from his hand as if it were a snake.

Tears sprang to Aggie's eyes as she watched her son she hardly knew stomp away. Falling to her knees in the snow, Aggie let out a whispered, desperate cry heavenward, "God of all Creation, please help my son. Do what it takes to rid his soul of the poison therein. Help me love him like You do."

From her weathered cheeks, her tears fell freely. She took the edge of her beautiful, rainbow scarf and dried her face. Taking a deep breath, Aggie rose from her knees and continued on with her day.

# CHAPTER 6

Leaving deep footprints in the snow Andrew stormed away from his home, knowing he had left his mother crying yet again. Natalia unknowingly set him off; her insistence that he get up out of his warm bed and get ready for work was all it took. It angered Andrew even more that it was affecting him so deeply today. In the past he could control his emotions and not be controlled by them, but lately he felt like a fire was constantly smoldering within his chest and it took only one piece of wood, one simple sentence, to set it ablaze again; today, her pushing him to be the man of the house was the large piece of kindling that fed his inner flame.

*Why do her words make me so angry? I am not the man of the house! My father should be, not me. Not then, not now! When I was a child, I had to be the man when he left on fishing excursions for a week at a time. Now I am to be the man because of his illness!* With these thoughts brewing, Andrew reached up and yanked a branch from a tree and threw it with all his might into the woods letting out a fierce yell of frustration.

Breathing hard, he began to pace the forest floor looking for an outlet for his rage. Shaking, Andrew finally sat down on a boulder, consciously making himself breathe deeply to calm down.

The images began again, the ones he hated most of all, like a story that one of the old Indians wouldn't stop re-telling.....

*A strange boat. Two white, nameless men. One a simple boatman, with a large frame, bushy beard, and dark eyes, earning his wages. One an explorer, tall, lean, neatly dressed, searching for and studying plants, herbs, and flowers to use for medicine. Little Andrew, five years old, left alone for two nights with his mother while his father was away fishing. Andrew couldn't understand nor stop what he saw. His mother's soft cries of pain and fear. The large boatman on top of his small mother, holding her down. Andrew caught sight of her tear-stained, pain-filled face and ran off into the night when the big man slapped her across the face to quiet her cries. Tree limbs raking across his little face as Andrew blindly ran into the woods alone, crying in his helplessness to do anything for his mother.*

Jumping up from the rock, his anger even now more aflame, Andrew took off at a dead run towards nothing, just *away* from the torment and pain in his soul, until the quiet sobbing of his mother subsided in his mind.

As Andrew ran, the scene that haunted his days and nights evaporated into others. Plans to leave Datka and find adventure and freedom from the life here his father wanted for him, fishing and trapping and carving a meager existence out of the Island for a family. This was not what he wanted, this hard life. He wanted more, like his friend Peter. In one more year, Andrew would be twenty-one like Peter, able to go where he wanted, buy what he wanted, have what he wanted. If he could only wait one more year for freedom.

\*\*\*\*\*\*\*\*\*\*\*\*\*\*\*\*\*\*\*\*

As one young man stormed away from his mother's home because of her encouragement to get up and go to work, another son of the same age cared nothing that he left his mother in the rainbow scarf behind in tears.

But these two boy-men had mothers at home, though hurt and heart-broken, with well-worn knees from constantly being bent in prayer on their sons' behalf.

# CHAPTER 7

Her head spinning with disbelief, Rose tried to sort out what was going on around her. In a matter of a half hour her brother and mother had gotten into a heated disagreement, and her aunt and cousin had parted ways on bad terms as well. The downside to living so closely to each other was that Rose knew what went on in most everyone's home around her.

She was deeply troubled at the anger and fury she saw both brother and cousin display. Rose wondered what in the world was going on to keep them so emotionally charged. These weren't the first outbursts she had witnessed.

Though Rose loved her big brother dearly and looked up to him, when she was younger she never felt a deep brother-sister connection with him like other siblings had. When they were younger, he always looked out for her. Around the age of five or six, Rose felt a shift in their relationship. Andrew seemed more distant and withdrawn from her, making Rose feel like she didn't belong or was in the way. Now he just basically ignored her presence and gave her only one or two word answers to her questions. When the missionaries used to come to the Islands, he would become angry when she would play with the missionaries and their children.  He would always leave when they came around and go find work to do.

When Rose was younger, she became increasingly aware of the differences between herself and the other Aleutian Indians.  Never quite able to pinpoint those differences, Rose would quickly dismiss those thoughts.  After just turning 16 last month, the old thoughts of being peculiar returned.  The starkest difference to Rose was her skin color.  Hers was a much lighter shade of brown than her family and friends.  Rose wished she were darker-skinned like the others though her friends admired her lighter skin tone.  She also had different colored eyes, a mix of green and gold with brown flecks.  All other Aleutians had rich, dark, brown eyes.  These differences never used to trouble her until this past year.  As her pre-teen years wore on, she hoped her friends would catch up with her in height, but they didn't. Her tall, slender frame was easily five inches above the others her age, earning her the nick-name "Tall Tree."

When she was a little girl, Rose asked her mother what her name meant and where it came from.  Her mother got a far away, pained look in her eyes then she took Rose to a small wooden box.  Inside the special box her mother had some treasured items:  a beaded necklace, a pair of tiny boots that

Rose and her brother both wore as babies, and other assorted keepsakes.

From the very bottom of the box, her mother lifted out a picture of a beautiful deep-red flower. The picture had been carefully torn from a book and folded several times to fit in the box. Rose's mother told her that it was a drawing of a flower she had never seen before, a rose. A white man had given the picture to her long ago. She told Rose he was an explorer, a botanist, someone who researched plants and herbs. This picture of the rose was in his special book.

When Rose inquired about the sharp, pointy extensions on such a beautiful flower, her mother told her of the botanist's explanation. She quoted his words from memory, "A rose is one of the most beautiful, sweet-smelling, flowers on earth. Its petals are velvety soft, as soft as a baby's cheek, with dark green leaves. The stem has very sharp points called 'thorns' that can hurt if you get pricked by one. The rose always reminds me that beauty can grow in the midst of pain." Rose's mother then quickly refolded the picture and whisked Rose outdoors towards another chore.

Not until last year did Rose begin to secretly wonder why her mother chose to name her after something that was so beautiful, yet a vivid reminder of pain as well. Questions swirled in her young mind, looking for answers she couldn't quite yet grasp. Rose was determined to one day find the answers believing they would unlock all of the mystery in her young heart bringing with it peace to the inner struggle within of who she was and where she belonged.

*********************

Natalia sat mending a torn place in her husband Ivan's seal-skin coat. She had watched as her beautiful Rose moved around the house that morning taking care of her and Ivan. Rose had worn a frown this morning, one like she had often worn lately, that showed she was deep in thought about something important. *What deep, important thoughts trouble my Rose today?* wondered Natalia. *She has been very inquisitive about her name again. I know I must tell her one day the whole story, but when, how? Is she old enough to know the truth?*

Natalia's own frown told of the condition of her thoughts as she sat mending. Rose, such a picture of sweetness and grace, yet a constant reminder of how life can hand you unexpected events, painful events, that are somehow overshadowed by pure, simple, beauty. As clearly as the day it happened, the images rushed to Natalia's mind....

*Two white men had traveled by boat to Datka Island. Ivan was away for several days of fishing, leaving her and young Andrew home alone. She hated being without her husband, but they needed the catch to meet their little family's needs.*

*Natalia watched as the boat came to shore and the two men disembarked. She had been with Andrew at the shoreline, getting him out of the house for a while to play. The men approached her, one brazen in his looks and stares, the other more of a gentleman. The gentleman introduced himself as Jacques, a French botanist who was on a mission looking for different medicinal herbs. He had hired the other, larger white man, Pierre, as his boatman and navigator.*

*Pierre made Natalia very uncomfortable. He didn't once speak to her, nor did he take his eyes off of her. Jacques asked if she would be willing to cook meals for them while they were on the island in return for money. She agreed, hesitantly, but knowing how much her family needed the money she decided to do this.*

*Jacques and Pierre had their own sleeping provisions with them, a tent designed for the freezing, wet temperatures of Alaska, which was fine with her. For two days the men came into her home and had three meals with her and Andrew. Jacques showed her his books that contained pictures of plants and flowers and trees she had never seen. She and Andrew were captivated by the botanist and his fervent enthusiasm for his work. He would even leave a book for her to look at during the day while he was away hunting for more plants.*

*On the third day, Natalia regretted for the rest of her life her decision to feed the men. Only one thing made the decision something she could live with. Jacques had finished his breakfast before anyone and went to gather the supplies for the day's work. Pierre got up from the meal and walked outside to leave; Little Andrew had gone off on some adventure.*

*Natalia began clearing away breakfast when she heard a noise behind her. Startled, she turned to see Pierre standing in the doorway. He closed the door behind him and walked towards her. "What do you need, Pierre?" Natalia could hear her quaking voice ask the question.*

*Saying nothing, he grabbed her arm and shoved her towards the bed. There he took advantage of her while she struggled to free herself from his iron-like grip, afraid he would kill her from the fierceness of his actions. She screamed once, but he quickly slapped her face and covered her mouth with his hand until she thought she would die from lack of air. When he was done, he left as quickly as he had appeared.*

*Shaking uncontrollably, Natalia got up and cleaned herself up as best as she could, knowing her body and mind and soul would never be the same. Natalia did not know what to do.*

*By the next day, Jacques unexpectedly announced that they needed to leave the island. She thanked God above for this as she watched Pierre load the boat with their supplies; never once did he come back to the house.*

Jacques came to the house to pay Natalia for the meals she had provided for them. He looked in her eyes for a moment, started to say something, then stopped. Jacques handed her the money he owed her. It was folded up in a piece of paper. All he said to her was "I hope this money will be enough for our time here. I enclosed it in a picture that I saw you looking at the other morning. It is a rose, one of the most beautiful, sweet-smelling, flowers on earth. Its petals are velvety soft, as soft as a baby's cheek, with dark green leaves. The stem has very sharp points called 'thorns' that can hurt if you get pricked by one. The rose always reminds me that beauty can grow in the midst of pain." He quickly turned and left. Natalia never saw the two men again.

# CHAPTER 8

With each overly loud tick of the wall clock, Gabe felt his frustrations mount as every second that passed seemed to mock him. *You have no job. You wasted your time and money at college. Your degree is useless. You have no future.*

Pushing himself up off his bed, knowing this was getting him nowhere, Gabe threw on a sweat shirt and sneakers and headed down the Parker's driveway to his familiar jogging route. Not normally given to discouragement and self-loathing, Gabe was troubled at the downward spiral of his thoughts. Running would help. It would clear his mind and let off some steam.

As he jogged, Gabe silently prayed. "God, help me get my head screwed back on straight. I know You have my future in hand. But honestly I'm a little confused at what You want from me. I know as a person I am more than a job or a degree. And I know I *need* a job to get by in life. Lead me, please. Help me see and know where to go, what to do."

His mind still whirling, as soon as Gabe's prayer ended, his thoughts drifted back to this morning.....

Gabe had spent the morning chasing job leads for the fourth week in a row again running into more dead-ends. On a whim he stopped for lunch at his old job where he used to deliver pizzas. Catching his eye like a neon sign, he saw posted in the window of the restaurant an ad that said, "Hiring: Pizza Delivery Driver."

*Great,* Gabe thought. *I asked for a sign and there it is. After today's success, I may as well apply for my old job.*

The smell of food reminded Gabe that he had survived the morning on two cups of coffee alone. *Well, here goes my last $2,* he grumbled. Planning on applying for the job after he ate lunch, Gabe ordered two slices of sausage pizza and a fountain drink. Needing some reprieve from the hustle and bustle of the morning, he found a quiet corner and started eating lunch. Two bites into his pizza, he heard a familiar female voice.

"Well, well, if it isn't my old friend, Gabe," purred Alicia, hands on her hips as she sauntered towards his table. Without waiting to be invited, Alicia made herself comfortable in the chair across from Gabe. "So what have you been up to? Haven't seen you around in quite awhile. How many *Indians* have you rescued lately from the horrors of their frozen little island?" The way she said the word "Indians" made Gabe's skin crawl and his nostrils flare.

Taking a deep breath before answering Alicia, he said, "I haven't been to Alaska in about three years. I went to junior college and got my associates, and now I am out job hunting." Hoping to change the subject, he asked, "How've you been?"

Alicia looked him up and down, liking what she saw. She reached over and picked up his last slice of pizza and took a delicate bite. "You don't mind, do you? Well, let's see." She paused for affect. "I just dumped my boyfriend and have my eye out for new prospects."

She finished the bite of pizza and pulled a napkin out of the holder. Alicia quickly wrote her phone number on it and slid it across the table towards Gabe. "Call me sometime, Gabe. Thanks for lunch."

When she saw that he didn't even reach for the napkin nor even acknowledge her invitation, Alicia looked him in the eyes and sneered, "You gave your heart away a long time ago, didn't you? To a bunch of helpless, stupid Indians in a frozen, dark world. Your loss." Plastering on her usual flirty smile and giving Gabe a quick little wave of her well-manicured fingers, she picked up her purse and coyly, quietly sang as she walked away, "One little, two little, three little Indians....." then burst out laughing at her own joke.

Forgetting about the sign in the window, Gabe quickly tossed his unfinished pizza and the napkin with Alicia's number in the trash and left the restaurant in worse shape than he arrived.

With every pound of his feet on the pavement, Gabe released the pent up anger he had stored from the conversation with Alicia. Gabe wasn't ignorant to the fact that most people didn't understand his love for the Aleutian people. He had faced that most of his life.

He just wasn't used to the disrespect and distaste that poured from Alicia's lips. He didn't need anyone to understand his desire to visit Alaska and serve the people there. He just wanted people to be decent and respectful especially if they knew nothing of what they were talking about. The Aleutians were some of the most honorable, brave, hard-working, caring, and compassionate people he had ever met.

With each passing thought Gabe realized how much he missed them. A lot had changed in his life in the three years since his last trip there. He had graduated from high school, gone to college, earned his Associate's degree in logistics, and worked a couple of different jobs. He hadn't realized how distracted he had been from missing several summers in Alaska until now. Memories of past mission trips flooded his mind.....

*Playing tag with the Aleutian Indian children. Teaching them to play simple games like jacks and how to use a yo-yo. His first sighting of aurora borealis, the Northern Lights. Eating seal meat for the first time. Learning to walk on snow shoes. Working alongside his own father and other missionary men with the Indian men on home improvements, patching a roof, and repairing a fishing boat. Watching with fascination as the young Indian girls helped their mothers weave baskets and tan animal hides for clothes and shoes.....*

Three years had been a long time to be gone. Gabe missed their easy smiles, their hearty laughter, and their willingness to help someone in need even though their own need was at times greater. *Will I ever return? How will a new employer like the idea of me taking off for three or more weeks at a time to go to Alaska? Or is that even a possibility when I get a job?*

Alicia's comment echoed through his mind. *"You gave your heart away a long time ago, didn't you? To a bunch of helpless, stupid Indians in a frozen, dark world."* His anger quickly returned at her words; feet still keeping a steady pace with his thoughts, Gabe pondered her ignorant comment for a bit.

Did his heart belong to the Aleutians, to missions in Alaska? He loved Washington, his hometown, his church, his family and friends, his life here, but why did there seem to be such an inner tug of war all of a sudden? Was Alaska pulling at him again? Suddenly Gabe saw clearly that it was! Yes,

yes, it was pulling at him to return. He *did* have a desire to go back, but when? How? All of this would have to wait until he had this job problem settled.

Gabe's pace began to slow, his thoughts slowing too. Now at a comfortable walk, he could hear the wind whispering in the tree-tops. The inner turmoil, for the moment, had settled. In its place, at first just a whisper like the wind, then quietly, but firmly, he felt the words blow across his heart.

*Be still and know that I am God.*

*Be still.*

Gabe strolled up his driveway a different person than when he left the house earlier. His body had expended itself of all of the pent up energy from the stress of the day, but mostly, the reassuring words and peace of God had filled his mind and heart bringing a settling and a calmness he hadn't felt in weeks.

# CHAPTER 9

Without warning the fire began, racing from branch to branch, tree to tree, then uncontrollably from roof-top to roof-top. Orange flames lit up the night sky. Shouts resounded in all directions, mothers screaming for children, children crying for mothers. At the midnight hour, above all a bell could be heard, signaling every able-bodied person to help in the rescue under way. Minds racing, everyone was wondering: *What had caused this fire to start? Did someone leave something too close to their evening heat source?*

Fires were a rarity on Datka Island. With the almost constant fog and rainy conditions, the Island stayed damp usually. An unusual lack of rain over the last month had allowed the Island to dry out considerably. That, coupled with the village's closely laid out homes and out-buildings, was a recipe for disaster. Part of the Aleutian Island chain, Datka Island was once an active volcano hundreds of years ago. The Aleutian Indians who eventually settled here built their homes on the one side of the island that was more accessible to the Alaskan mainland and also where there was more available land for homes near the shoreline. The set up was perfect for the small community that carved out their livelihood in trapping and fishing. But the one thing that made their community strong also fueled the fire that destroyed part of this little Island. The fire had quickly consumed seven homes and the on-shore boat shed that held five fishing boats. The school was on the outskirts of these seven destroyed homes and the fire's destructive tentacles reached it as well.

Panic spread through Datka Island's inhabitants as quickly as the tentacles of the fire. Disbelief and confusion made legs and minds freeze at the sights and sounds before them. Slowly reality took over the minds of some of the people as the men began shouting orders to form an assembly line of sorts to put out the fire. Children and mothers found each other, some began grabbing all of the belongings they could carry from their small homes and carrying their precious belongings to safety.

Minds and arms and legs began to respond to the scene now, taking action to save their homes. Buckets and pails of water travelled down an assembly line of arms and hands to each structure in danger. Though it seemed like forever, within several hours the fires were at least contained. Thankfully, no one was harmed, just a few minor burns from fighting the fires. The community knew that many more homes could have been lost and much more destruction could have happened. Seeing the charred remains of the fishermen's boats that were stored at the community's boat shed on shore brought the stark reality that some of their livelihoods had just gone up in flames. At least the school had suffered only minor damages and was not in ruins. A hush had settled over the area where the fire had been. All were simply relieved that no lives were lost, or serious injuries inflicted.

After damages were quickly assessed, Datka's people stood with sweat and tear-streaked, soot-covered faces, again almost paralyzed from the suddenness and unbelief and exhaustion of the last couple of hours. One by one the silent tears began to be quiet sobs and even low moans as a few realized they had lost their entire home and belongings. Men and women alike comforted those mourning their losses with a tender hug and reassuring words that as a people they would get through this together.

Seeing the immediate need for everyone to eat, drink, and rest a while before sunup, Rose's Aunt Aggie jumped into action. With some of the men still putting out and watching smoldering areas, she took charge of the situation. As an elderly, respected woman in the village Aggie knew they would listen to her.

She looked into the soot-marked faces of her community and began assigning people who had lost their homes to ones who hadn't, gathering extra blankets, furs, and robes for the night. She hurriedly made sure that all had a place to lay their heads and a quick meal before bed. With about 3 hours left to sleep, Aggie knew they all needed to take advantage of the late-rising sun and try to rest, knowing at sun-up the hard work would begin.

Some still stood around bewildered at what had just happened, unsure of what to do next. Aggie's quick thinking and planning helped spring-board everyone else into action for the remainder of the dark hours until sunrise. She spoke firmly, but gently to all in earshot. "Brothers and sisters, we need a few hours rest while the smoldering areas cool off before work can begin. Please, let's all return home, make sure those in need have a warm bed for the night and tomorrow we will meet as one and distribute to the ones who have lost their homes and belongings. Let's lay our heads down with thankful hearts that no lives were lost."

Slowly the group began to disperse, arms around those still in shock from losing homes and possessions, guiding them to a safe haven for the evening.

*********************

During the assessment of damages and the group meeting, Rose and her best friend, Luka, had blended into the shadows, clinging to each other, trembling from head to toe. Both were bewildered at what they had witnessed, hoping their eyes had played tricks on them.

Both of the girls' homes were located the farthest from where the fires had begun. At the sound of the bell the girls had left their houses and headed to assist in any way they could. Each girl saw the other and grabbed hands running towards the burning structures.

Rose's aunt sent both back to find more buckets, pots, pails, anything that could hold a large amount of water. Hand in hand, they took a short cut through the trees towards the backs of their homes to locate buckets.

As quickly and silently as two hares, the girls ran through the trees, reached a curve in the path, and came upon four figures huddled together with their backs to Rose and Luka. Not knowing who the four figures were, the girls quickly hid. Upon hearing the voices, Rose and Luka were able to identify them: Rose's brother Andrew, Luka's brother Markus, Rose's cousin Joshua, and Peter, who both girls barely knew. The four men were speaking to each other in fearful, hushed tones.

"Look what you've done!" Luka heard her brother's voice.

"We have to go help!" Andrew cried.

"We can't! No one can know we did this or we will pay dearly." Joshua was panicking also as the reality of their actions set in.

"That's my father's boat on fire; I have to help!" Andrew was now desperate to do something, anything.

His friends held him back and continued to reason with Andrew. "This is all your fault! You can't go running up to help put out the fire you caused," one of the men hissed.

"I didn't mean for it to happen this way. I just wanted to play a joke on our girlfriends, just shake them up a bit," Andrew hissed.

"Well you did that! Your little '*joke*' caused all of this! I warned you not to do it!" The one speaking then shoved Andrew hard which in turn made him even more angry and frightened. Andrew shoved back and a scuffle ensued among three of the four. As men began heading their way in search of anything to help put out the fire, the fourth young man quickly got his three partners' attention and harshly whispered, "Someone's coming! Run!" The four flew by Rose and Luka without seeing them, leaving a wave of the strong smell of alcohol in their wake.

Luka cried, "Rose, what do we do? Our own brothers did this!"

Rose's fear-filled eyes looked into her best friend's face. "I don't know, Luka. Say nothing for now. We have to go help put out this fire!"

The two girls took off faster than ever intent on trying to undo the horrific damage partly caused by their own two brothers.

# CHAPTER 10

The Parker's phone rang early in the morning bringing Rand and Becca out of a deep sleep. Grabbing the phone by his bed table, Rand answered.

"Hello?"

"Randall Parker? Is that you?"

"Yes, this is Randall. Who's speaking?"

"Rand, this is Stuart Brooks with the Alaska Missionaries Relief Aid. I'm sorry to call so early but we have a situation that I hope you can help us with."

At the word "Alaska" Rand was now fully awake. "Hi, Stuart! Fill me in and we will see what can be done."

Becca yawned and propped up on pillows listening to Rand's end of the conversation.

"Three days ago there was a fire on Datka Island that destroyed seven homes and some fishing boats. No injuries, only minor burns to a few. Thankfully, no deaths either. Word got to one of our mission friends in Southwest Alaska, and he called me immediately to see when our next trip there was planned. I know we are still a good two months away from heading back to Alaska. Truthfully I was going to either have to postpone for two additional months or not go at all. My mother is very ill and I need to go stay with her for a while; I'm planning to be gone four to six months. I just can't pull off the organizing and traveling for this relief trip right now. That's where you come in, I hope."

Rand replied, "Wow! I'm sorry to hear that about the fire and about your mother. Stuart, so many of our long-time friends live there. We have devoted most of our mission work to the people of Datka Island. Can you tell me about any of them in particular?" Rand took a deep breath trying to calm his heart. *God, be with our friends*, he quietly prayed.

Stuart answered, "Rand, I am sorry, but I wasn't given any names or details that might be helpful to you. I only have information from an outside source that reached us at AMRA. I will pray for your friends."

"I understand, Stuart. Give me today to talk to Becca and our schools to see if there's a possibility of us leaving so soon. I will call you first thing in the morning."

"Sounds good, Rand. How's that son of yours? I haven't seen him in several years. I bet he's a grown man by now."

"Gabe just finished getting his logistics degree and is now job hunting. He's not having much success, but something will turn up."

"Logistics?!? Rand, that's exactly what we need for this mission! I am the logistics guy for these trips and since I won't be here after next week, I have really been worried about that end of things. What would you think of me asking your son to help in this area? If anyone would know, you would. Would Gabe be capable of such a task? He won't be working alone but will be teamed up with another AMRA director. With him not yet finding a job, maybe God had this situation in mind for Gabe."

Rand quickly responded, "If he is working with someone on this project I think Gabe could handle it. Maybe I should have him talk to you and get more details on the job's specific duties, then you will know if Gabe's the man for the project."

"Sounds good. Give him my number and I will speak with him tomorrow while you and Becca work out details with your jobs. Talk to you soon, Rand. God bless. Bye."

Rand hung up and shook his head in wonder. "Becca, you won't believe this."

"What, Rand? Are our Aleutian friends okay? It sounded bad." Worry creased her brow. These precious ones were like a part of their family and she couldn't bear the thought of any of them suffering. Quickly tears sprang to her eyes.

Placing a hand on her arm, Rand replied, "Yes, honey, everyone's okay. There was a fire with some homes and boats destroyed but no lives lost, thank God. We don't know any more details at this time. The need is of course great and immediate." Rand finished filling her in on his conversation with Stuart.

Becca took a deep breath after hearing that no lives were lost and everyone was safe. Her heart grieved for the loss of their homes and possessions, knowing how very priceless the Aleutians' few belongings were to them.

When he told her of the logistics need, she laid a small hand on her chest to still her pounding heart. "Oh, Rand. Their needs will be so very great. So much has been lost." Her voice caught in her throat, stopping her words." After a moment of silence, something occurred to Becca. "Rand, I wonder if God has had Gabe in mind for just this opportunity and that's why he has been unable to find a job. He will be needed to fill Stuart's shoes in the logistics area and to help our dear friends." Becca slowly smiled, "And he only thought his degree was a waste."

# CHAPTER 11

*Ear-splitting cracking, like that of a rifle shot at close range....several more loud cracks, then that same piercing scream, a girl's voice, a girl's hand, so close but out of his grasp...*

Analyzing this same recurring dream was doing nothing for Gabe but leaving him with the beginnings of a splitting headache. *Why do I keep having this dream? This premonition that someone needs my help? How can I help a faceless person, someone I can't even identify?*

Pushing aside the early morning fogginess of mind, Gabe decided sleep wasn't going to reclaim him, at least dreamless sleep anyway. Not wanting to re-enter such a confusing state of mind, he headed for the shower.

After dressing for his day of job-hunting that lie ahead, Gabe reached for his Bible on the night table. Quickly, quietly he prayed. *"God, show me something in Your Word to calm my mind and heart. This dream, the job hunt, my future....it all seems too much right now."* He flipped his Bible open and looked at the page before him at verses he had read a few mornings ago. Philippians 4:6 leapt off the page at him once again.

*"Be anxious for nothing, but in everything by prayer and*

*supplication, with thanksgiving, let your requests be made known to God."*

Gabe flipped over a few more pages and read on.

*"Count it all joy when you fall into various trials, knowing that the testing of your faith produces patience."*

James 1:2-3 was even more brutal than the passage in Philippians. Knowing God always knew just what he needed to hear, Gabe took these passages to heart. Aloud and alone in his room, Gabe did something very familiar to himself, he prayed aloud, just talked to God as if He were sitting across from him. "God, I hear You, but I am having a hard time doing it. Rejoice and be joyful is what I am hearing but not what I am feeling. I know my feelings aren't trustworthy, but You and Your Word are. So right now, I choose to be joyful today, no matter what today holds. Help me; lead me. Amen."

Gabe then headed down to the kitchen to start the coffee pot and saw that both of his parents were already having an early morning cup. "You guys are up early. Did I wake you?" Gabe asked Rand and Becca.

"No, Son. The phone woke us up about an hour ago. I was afraid we would bother you."

Gabe reached for a mug and filled it with steaming coffee. He leaned down to squeeze his mother's shoulders and noticed the smirk she was trying to hide. "What's got you so happy this morning, Mom?"

"Oh, nothing. Want a muffin?" She handed her tall, handsome son a blueberry muffin which he quickly accepted. "So why can't you sleep, sweetie?" Becca asked Gabe.

"Let's just say a dream woke me up. Who called so early? Is everything okay?" Gabe joined his parents at the table.

A slightly older version of Gabe, Rand looked up at his son. "Stuart Brooks with the Alaska Missionaries Relief Aid called."

Gabe's eyebrows shot up. "Really? What's up? He doesn't just call to chat."

"It sounds like a fire broke out on the Island and some homes, the school, and some boats were destroyed or damaged. No one was hurt, thank goodness, but needless to say, there are great needs for some of the families and the school needs extensive repairs."

"Wow! How could a fire start there? That's so unusual for fire to spread due to the fog and rainy conditions."

"We don't have any details on how it started, just the damages. The problem is Stuart has to be gone from the mission center for several months due to his mother's illness so...."

Becca couldn't contain herself any longer. She grabbed Gabe's hands across the table and blurted out, "So he needs a logistics guy to plan for the relief trip to Alaska!"

Gabe slumped back in his seat while both his parents watched the emotions cross his face. First confusion, then slowly the realization of what they were saying, and then a slow smile came next, followed by a deep frown of concentration as they knew he was already formulating a plan.

Immediately Gabe froze mid-thought. "Wait a minute. Is this why I haven't been able to find a job? God knew He needed me elsewhere?" Gabe did something he hadn't done in a while; he laughed. It began with an uncontrollable chuckle that turned into true merriment. "And all this time I was fretting over something I wasn't supposed to have in the first place."

Rand stood from the table and replied, "I think you have a phone call to make."

*******************

Head spinning from all of the changes that had taken place in the span of 2 short hours, Gabe picked up the phone and called his best friend Ed. "Hey, buddy. We're throwing burgers on the grill tonight. Want to join us? Plus I have an ulterior motive to this dinner invitation that I'll explain later if you can make it."

"You've definitely got my attention! Is Mrs. Bee making her brownies?" Ed asked with a chuckle.

"I'll see what strings I can pull. See you at 6:00." Gabe ended his call with Ed and stared at the notes in front of him he had written during his phone call with Stuart.

- *Fire on the island - source unknown*
- *Seven homes, boats, school destroyed or damaged*
- *Stu not available to go for relief trip*
- *Resupply homes and families' needs*
- *Construction work on school*
- *Boats replaced or repaired*
- *Time frame: 1-arrive in Juneau at AMRA for planning, 2-leave within 2 weeks or sooner for Island, 3-stay 2-3 months at least*
- *Be in charge of logistics for trip, work with John Miller with AMRA*
- *Ed and parents go too?*

At the bottom of his notes, Gabe quickly scrawled a portion of a verse that came to mind. "For I know the plans I have for you..." The reality of this promise was sinking in minute by minute. Gabe was slowly beginning to see the interweaving of the threads of his life coming together and making some sense. As a boy, his love for the Aleutian people, his differences in interests from others his age, his love for the outdoors, his ability to plan and manage a situation, his logistics degree, even his lack of a job....all seeming to fit together somehow and become an intricate, God-planned tapestry of his life.

A sense of peace and joy filled his heart, something that had eluded him these last few months if not longer. Gabe was beginning to trust, really trust, a deep-down, unshakeable measure of trust in God like he had never had before. Maybe that trust was the source of this peace and joy he had found.

Some serious changes were about to take place in his world. He knew this trust would see him through the days to come.

# CHAPTER 12

Rubbing the soft ears of her pet Malamute Stormy, Rose inhaled deeply the morning air. Stormy was more than just a sled dog for Rose and her family. She was like a family member. Rose bent down and briefly buried her face in Stormy's thick, sable coat. Rose stood and stretched her long body; then she and her pet set out for a morning walk to the shoreline. Still tinged with the scent of burned down sedges, trees, and homes nearby her own, the scent reminded her of the hard days to come. Rose worried about what was to be done for these hurting families that had recently lost so much. Living on the island had its advantages and disadvantages. Surrounded by nature and family and friends, the simpler life wasn't always the easier life. Supplies and necessities for the families in need weren't exactly close by, nor did they have enough money to purchase them.

Pride filled Rose's chest as she thought of how the families whose homes were spared had pulled together and taken in and cared for the families that had no home. On Datka Island, as well as on the other Aleutian Islands, blood ties and family bonds were inseparable. When crises arose, there was never a doubt that help was close by.

Her thoughts quickly turned to Yuri, a single man who had lost both parents and his sister to pneumonia. He lived alone with room to spare and was more than willing to open his home up to a family in need. Michael and Lydia, a young couple with one daughter, Lillian, and Lydia's aging mother, Ola, now filled Yuri's home to capacity. He was gone most of the daylight hours trapping and fishing. Yuri seemed pleased to have family around him again, also to have women cook for him, something he had greatly missed since the passing of his own mother and sister.

Rose had heard this morning that a trip was being planned by some of the men to make a boat trip to Seal Harbor for the most essential needs. They would take dried salmon, furs, baskets, clothing, and other wanted items to sell to the tourist shops to purchase their needed things. Hopefully, the buyers at Seal Harbor would be generous. With tourism season several months away, this was risky but worth a try.

Walks with Stormy allowed time for Rose to reflect. Thinking back, Rose remembered that as a young girl, she had traveled with her father by boat to Seal Harbor to purchase some much needed items for their own home and his fishing business. The harbor town had frightened her with all the noise and the hustle and bustle of the townspeople. She was overwhelmed with the sights, smells, and sounds around her. Excited from the variety of items in the store from candy to kayaks, bolts of material to hammers, huge bags of coffee and pouches of dried tobacco, her stomach reeled with the smells around her and the uncontrollable giddiness she was experiencing. The streets were littered with drunken men and women alike, discarded bottles of liquor, and other trash as well. The scantily clad women would look at her with disdain in their eyes, reality and sadness overwhelming them that their own youthful days were now over. Rose stayed as close to her father's side as she could get and held tightly to his hand.

They shared a lunch of bread and hard cheese and some dried, salty meat she had never had before and a bottle of soda. The soda was her favorite thing of the day. She liked the way it tickled her throat going down. Leaving the town and heading back to her home of Datka Island, Rose knew that even if she was able to have one soda a day all to herself and have to live in town to get it, she would definitely decline the trade of town life with island life. The smells and sights of town drifting slowly away behind their boat gave way to the things she loved most. In its place she enjoyed the returning quiet, clean air, the plenteous wildlife both on water and land, and the sense of peace and safety of her island.

Now at 16, Rose could see the pull the town had on her brother and his friends, both male and female. She often heard them complaining of how boring and dead Datka Island was compared to Seal Harbor. Gambling and drinking had a strong grip on the up and coming generation. They were clearly taken with the pool and gambling halls, the bars, and the stark differences of life there. Rose hoped and believed when she grew older she wouldn't be distracted by that kind of life. A part of her felt sorry for her older sibling, her cousins, and friends. What *did* the island have to offer but for them to carry on in their parents' footsteps? If you didn't have a desire to fish or trap animals or weave baskets or sew items to sell to tourists, there wasn't much else in their future. But alcohol, gambling, and wasting your life away wasn't the answer either.

Her head swam with questions that demanded answers. *What does my future hold? In 5 or 10 years what will I be doing? Married with children, sewing and weaving like my mother and aunt? Creating a life out of the island for myself as a single young woman, but doing what? Oh, to be young again! I never worried about the future when I was young. Now it haunts me!*

As the word "haunts" flitted across her mind, so did something else that haunted her often. The dream, the big black book, the blue clad angel-man. *What was in that book?*

*Why does it call to me at night in my dreams and at the same time strike such horrifying fear in my heart? Who is the mysterious man in my dreams?*

Rose and Stormy reached the shoreline. She picked up a smooth rock and tossed it in the water watching the ripples it created. Her dear grandfather had once stood on this very shore and taught her to skip rocks. He also told her something she would never forget. Rose remembered his quiet words.....

*"Rose, do you see this rock? It is very small compared to the great water in front of you. But do you know this small rock can affect the great waters? If I toss this little rock in the water, it will create such an affect that it will go on and on and on."*

*"No it won't, Grandfather. If you throw the rock in, it will just sink to the bottom and lay there."*

*"Watch, Little One and tell me what you see."* Grandfather tossed the rock in and immediately the first ripple formed, then the second, then the third, and so on, until Little Rose lost count. She watched in amazement as the rings formed and grew outward from the toss of one small rock.

*"I see rings in the water where the rock went in. It did change the water, Grandfather! The rings keep going and going."*

*"Yes, Rose. You do see. Remember this: your actions are like a rock. They cause a ripple-affect and reach those around you. You, Rose, are like a rock thrown into the water. Wherever you land, you cause an affect that goes on and on and on like the ripples. Your life just doesn't end up somewhere and fall to the bottom like the rock. Know that your life will cause rings and ripples that will touch those around you."*

Rose skipped a few more rocks across the surface of the water. She then tossed in a few and watched the growing rings and wondered if one day, she really would touch the lives of those around her in a great way.

# CHAPTER 13

Coming out of her reverie, Rose called Stormy back to her side for their walk home. Pondering the events of the last few days, she could clearly see the affects of her brother, cousin, and their friends' actions. The ripples their actions had caused were affecting and touching many in their village, but not in a positive way. Would they survive the aftermath of these ripples? She was scared and angry at what she saw around her, the devastation they caused, all for foolish fun.

Rose headed down the well-worn path. As she was walking her foot slipped on something almost making her fall. After regaining her footing, Rose kicked around in the leaves and saw the brown glass bottle that had made her slip. She picked it up and immediately recognized the sickening aroma of liquor she had so often smelled on her brother as of late. She began to look around and notice a couple more of the same ones. She followed the trail of bottles towards an old two room house that had long been forgotten on the island. Walking towards it, Rose heard laughter coming from inside which nearly frightened her to death. No one had been in that house in years to her knowledge. She hid behind a group of sedges and listened. More laughter and male and female voices floated out of the cracked windows, then distinct, distinguishable, familiar voices carried to her ears. It was Andrew, Markus, Joshua, and some friends of theirs.

The longer Rose listened the angrier she became. She snuck up to one of the windows and peered in. Inside one of the rooms she saw the boys, each with a girl hanging onto them and the floor strewn with empty bottles. The boys were playing cards and drinking; the girls hanging on them, kissing and whispering in their ears. She saw a pile of money on the table too.

Rose heard a noise from the other room and crept to that window to peer in. Quickly she ducked back down, blushing at the sight of the couple on the old mattress. Rose had never seen such sights before, sickening her at the behavior of the boys she did know and the girls not much older than herself. Though close to Rose's age, they appeared years older with their painted faces and clothes that barely covered their bodies. Their language and actions were such that Rose couldn't stand to endure another moment.

She crouched down low and crept back the way she had come, tears burning her hazel eyes. Before reaching the path, she heard her name whispered loud enough for her to hear. *"Rose."*

Startled she looked up to see Luka behind a low-standing tree waving fiercely for Rose to join her. Rose scurried over to Luka and fell against her friend's shoulder, bursting into tears instantly. "Rose, hush now. Let's get farther away so we can talk."

Walking hand in hand they headed to a safer spot in the woods and sat down on a large boulder. Luka turned to Rose and hugged her. "Rose, I know what you saw. I got there awhile before you. I tried to get your attention before you got to the house but you didn't hear me. Our brothers' actions are getting worse! What are we going to do?" Tears sprang to Luka's eyes as well. Quickly she went on. "Those girls are from Seal Harbor. Markus and Andrew were talking last night about picking them up today and meeting at an old house. I heard them when Andrew came over around midnight. They sat outside by the fire and thought I was asleep. I snuck out to listen to them and heard their plan. These girls are not good, Rose. They sell their bodies to men for alcohol, money and even a meal. Our brothers usually pay them with food and alcohol to come to the island for a couple of days, but now the girls are demanding a higher price today. They want money too."

Rose shook her head, even more confused and bewildered at all of this information. "Luka, how do you know these things? What do you mean 'usually'? This isn't the first time for them to come here?"

Luka shook her head sadly. "I have spent the last week sneaking and watching the boys before I said anything. I didn't want to believe it, Rose. Not our brothers! I have followed them here several times and saw them bring the girls, feed them, give them liquor, then have their way with them. The next day they take them back to the harbor until they can 'pay' for them to come again. I don't know what to do, Rose, but something has to be done."

"Luka, what can we do? They are grown men, though acting like foolish, selfish children! No one can stop them."

Luka said nothing for a moment. "Rose, you haven't heard the worst of it yet."

Tears pooled again in Rose's eyes. She breathed a deep breath and shuddered at what else Luka had to say that could be even more horrific. "Tell me, Luka."

# CHAPTER 14

Curiosity was about to get the best of him as Ed parked his pick-up at the Parkers' home. Gabe's "ulterior motive" had been eating on him all day. *What on earth could Gabe have up his sleeve?* Ed wondered as he unfolded his long frame from his truck and bounded up the front steps. With a quick knock, he entered the house and headed straight for the kitchen.

Becca was mixing up something chocolate, hopefully her brownies. Ed snuck up behind her and quickly pecked her on the cheek. "Hey, Mrs. Bee!" While she was distracted he stuck a finger in her bowl and licked it off. "Mmmmm. You're the best! You're making brownies."

"Oh so now I know why you think I'm the best. It's all about the brownies," she teased.

Ed flashed his half-grin at Becca and said, "And your mashed potatoes, and homemade rolls, and chocolate chip cookies…" She grabbed a hand towel from the counter and swatted at Ed. He ducked away just in time and headed out the back door.

"I think I hear Rand calling me," he said, with a quick wink.

Becca laughed to herself at Ed's humor. Though he had only been in their lives for four years, she was grateful that

God had led Ed to them. Not able to have any more children after Gabe, Becca now thought of Ed as another son. She loved how he and Gabe were like brothers, something her son had always longed for.

After Gabe's run-in outside the bar with Ed, things changed drastically and quickly for the young man. Ed's rough exterior and fake identification to get into the bars were traded for a more tidy appearance and time spent in church.

Just after high school graduation and the boys' first meeting, within two short months Ed went on his first mission trip to Alaska with the Parkers and another the following summer. He loved these trips almost as much as the Parkers did, and now if things worked out as Gabe had planned, Ed was in for another adventure. She was proud of both Ed and Gabe for spending the last few summers in junior college earning their degrees. Since Ed hadn't returned to Alaska since Gabe's last trip almost three years ago, Becca felt sure Ed would be nearly as excited about this as they all were.

Becca heard Gabe drive up just as she finished making the hamburger patties. Her tall son, who looked so much like Randall at that age, gave Becca a hug. "How's my favorite mom?"

"Better, now that all my boys are home. Your Dad and

Ed's getting the grill lit. Are you planning on talking to Ed about your plan tonight?"

"Yeah, but not until after dinner. I thought I would torture him a while longer." Gabe chuckled and headed outside with the men.

Father and son hugged, then the two friends shook hands. "Everybody have a good day?" Gabe asked both of them.

Rand spoke first. "My students were restless and hyper today. I think they all have Spring Break Fever. It can't get here soon enough."

"Sorry, Dad. You know how it is every March around this time. Hang in there." Gabe looked to Ed. "What about you, Bud?"

"Well, other than the suspense that's been threatening to kill me, I've had a great day!" Ed gave Gabe a friendly punch in the arm.

Gabe flopped down in a close by lounge chair with a big smile in place. Ed drawled, "Well somebody must have found a new job. You're grinning like a possum!"

"Nope. I'm still as jobless as I was yesterday," Gabe smirked.

"So why the big goofy grin? What's up?"

"Just at peace again, that's all." Gabe stretched his arms over his head and interlaced his fingers behind his neck to relax.

"When do I get details? Does it have to do with this news that you seem to be enjoying withholding from your best bud?" Ed was starting to get a bit annoyed with Gabe. He didn't like secrets.

"Maybe....Oh, Mom's calling, got to go help her get dinner ready." With that, Gabe jumped up and ran inside letting the screened door slam behind him.

Ed turned to Rand, "Did you hear Mrs. Bee? I didn't hear anybody. Or is he just messing with me?"

Rand laughed good-humoredly at Ed's discomfort. "Trust me, Ed. He will clue you in later. I promised not to let his news leak out. Gabe will tell you soon enough. Maybe a couple of burgers will distract you for a while. I'll go see if they have them ready to grill." Rand headed for the house leaving Ed stewing in his chair.

********************

As soon as Ed had swallowed his last bite of burger and wiped his mouth, he blurted, "Okay, Buddy, the wait is over. Details, details! I won't share the brownies if you don't share your news."

Gabe chuckled. "Fair enough, Ed. I told you earlier that I hadn't found a job but in a sense, I did. Our friend, Stuart Brooks, from the Alaska Missionaries Relief Aid called and there is an immediate, great need for someone to head up a relief trip to Datka Island. A fire destroyed some homes and boats and damaged the school. The man usually in charge of all logistical planning can't go because of a sick parent. Dad happened to mention that logistics is my specialty and Stuart invited me to take his place in this arena of the trip. I'll be working with John Miller, someone on the AMRA board I've never met."

"That's great news, Bud! Well, not for the Aleutians, but for you. See, God knew all along that a job would just get in the way of His plan for you."

"I agree, Ed. I see that now in hind-sight. The catch is I have to leave in a week for AMRA in Fairbanks to plan the relief trip, and I will probably be gone until the end of summer, for four to six months. Mom and Dad were asked to come too. That's where you come in, Ed. I could really use you on this trip too. That's my ulterior motive for having you for dinner, to try and talk you into traveling with me and

Mom and Dad for three weeks and you to fly back with them."

"Wow! You know how much I love these trips. It's been several years since we both went. It does sound like there's a great need for workers. But I have the opposite problem as you had. I have a job and a boss to consider. Let me think about it and let you know tomorrow." Ed leaned back in his chair, wheels already turning in his mind on how to possibly work out such an adventure. He truly loved the few trips he had been on with the Parkers. More importantly, he loved working on such projects to simply help others.

Rand spoke up. "Ed, Becca and I have talked to our school administrator about this trip. Since Spring Break is a week away, and that's when we need to leave, one of the three weeks for the trip will be during the break, so technically we only need two weeks off at school. There's about half a dozen substitute teachers for the school and we have claimed two of them. I took the liberty of putting a bug in the administrator's ear that you might want off as well for this trip. In his opinion, the head coach can handle things for two weeks if you decide you want to go with us. I'm not trying to tell you what to do, just making a suggestion."

Ed grinned and sat back quietly for a moment. "Well, since it seems to be okay with the school, I don't think I'll pass up the opportunity. Sounds like an adventure to me! Tomorrow I'll go to the school and make it official. Gabe, this is so far off the radar of what I thought we would be talking about tonight. I must say, I like your ulterior motives. Let's go to Alaska!"

********************

The next week flew by in a blur for Gabe, Rand, Becca, and Ed. Every spare moment was filled with making phone calls, packing, ordering plane tickets, working on lesson plans for the substitute teachers, and purchasing items for the trip to Fairbanks. They would fly there first for four days and help in any way they could to prepare for the two and a half week trip to Datka Island and their beloved Aleutians. Excitement grew in each of them at what God had in store for them to do.

Gabe did as much logistical planning as he could during the week at home so he wouldn't waste one second during the four days in Fairbanks. He knew his days there would need to be spent gathering supplies and tools and the much needed items for their friends. He also knew he needed wisdom from God for this trip. Being one of the people in charge was exciting and daunting at the same time. This was a mission he couldn't mess up.  Too much was at stake and he knew it.

# CHAPTER 15

*March, 1968*

About ten minutes prior to descending, Randall looked away from the tiny window that gave him a view of the Alaskan landscape. What he saw below was both familiar and breath-taking. From the fjords to the rocky coastlines, the sedges and low trees to the beautiful variety of birds, Rand loved coming to Alaska. The immense diversity in the landscape intrigued him every time he traveled there. Turning to Gabe, he asked, "Son, who did you say is meeting us at the airport?"

Gabe roused from his own thoughts, looked at his father, and answered, "John and Jill Miller from AMRA. John is one of the directors on the mission board who is taking Stuart's place. I will be working directly with him in planning the relief trip. He and his wife are about you and Mom's age. They have a twenty year old daughter, but I forget her name. They've never been to Datka Island but have travelled to other small Aleutian Islands. I know the couple has worked with Stuart for the last few years in Alaska. They've been active in the mission field for about twenty years but recently felt called to Alaska."

Becca looked up from her magazine. "I'm looking forward to meeting them. It's always nice to work with other women to brainstorm with on these types of trips."

Gabe answered her, "That's true, Mom. I will really be picking you ladies' brains about the household needs for the fire victims. You all will be a great asset to me and John. Dad, I'm thinking you and Ed will be most helpful in heading up the tools and construction needs for rebuilding the homes and working on the school. You both are experienced in this area."

Even while seated, Ed's legs were jumping with excitement. "Sounds good to me, Bro. Put me to use wherever you need me."

The pilot notified them to buckle their seat belts as he was preparing to land the plane. After a non-eventful landing, Rand and Becca, Gabe and Ed gathered their carry-on bags and disembarked from the small plane onto the private runway.

Gabe could see three people walking towards them and assumed it was the Millers. John and Jill were both dark-haired, no nonsense, efficient-looking man and wife in their mid 50's, both trim and athletic; he could tell they were accustomed to hard work. Walking beside Jill was a young woman, short and athletically-built like her parents with glossy, jet black, wavy hair, and even from this distance Gabe could see her eyes were a shade of green that made you look twice. She wore an engaging, easy smile and walked with a confidence that exuded from her body. Gabe gave a quiet, low whistle and spoke softly under his breath so only Ed could hear, "God sure knew what He was doing when He created that one."

Ed was rendered speechless, something that happened very rarely. Since he had first caught sight of the young lady, his jaw had slightly dropped, eyes staring as she approached them.

Gabe leaned towards his friend. "Close your mouth, Buddy. You're about to drool on your favorite pearl-snap shirt."

Ed snapped his jaw closed then muttered to Gabe, "I'm gonna marry her one day."

Gabe had never seen Ed show any interest in females before in quite this way. His eyes twinkled with unuttered laughter which he quickly concealed as they approached the Millers.

Stopping in front of John, Gabe extended his hand. "You must be John Miller. I'm Gabriel Parker; everyone calls me Gabe. This is my father Randall and mother Rebecca." He turned to Ed. "This is Ed Hamilton, my right hand man."

"Hi, Gabe." Jim shook hands with them all and began introductions. "This is my wife Jill and daughter Jade. You all must be exhausted. I bet it's been a busy week preparing for this trip. Let's grab your luggage and get some dinner."

The young lady's name fit her eye color perfectly. Her natural beauty was accentuated by her black, wavy hair and jade-green eyes. She reached for a cross hanging around her neck by a leather cord, made of the very green stone she was named after. The young beauty stopped fiddling with her necklace and spoke to the group, "Nice to meet you all. We look forward to working with each of you."

His parents and Ed each shook hands with the Millers then they all headed to help gather the luggage.

# CHAPTER 16

Unsure of where to start, Luka simply blurted out the sad truth for Rose to hear. Luka knew there was no possible way to soften it, nor could she protect her friend from it. "Our good-for-nothing brothers have been stealing! Think about it, Rose; where are they getting money for alcohol and food when they both barely work?" She paused to let it sink in for Rose. "They both are stealing from our parents! I heard mother and father talking about some money missing from father's pouch. They both think father dropped or mislaid it. I actually saw Markus with father's pouch. I asked him what he was doing, and he said he found it lying on the floor and was putting it on the shelf for father. At first, I believed him, but now I *know* he took some money from father."

Rose blanched as the truth hit her like a ton of boulders. She felt like she was smothering under a mound of blankets and furs that she couldn't free herself from. "Not Markus! He is always so good and helpful and true to his family. Maybe you are mistaken, Luka." Rose began to breathe heavily from the weight of her friend's words. She felt as if her world was falling in upon her.

"No, Rose, I'm not. I can't deny it any longer. The boys aren't getting better, but worse and now with this new discovery of the girls, them stealing, their drinking, and the fire, I can't hide this another moment, Rose! What destruction will happen next at their hands?" Luka was as much panic-stricken as Rose, but she could see clearly what she had to do, even if it involved her brother and her best friend's brother.

"Luka, what are you going to do? You can't tell! You just can't! Markus will end up in jail! He's your brother! And you can't tell anyone about who started the fire. There has been enough destruction. Don't you see, the knowledge will destroy both of our parents, too?"

Luka sighed deeply. "Rose, I have thought about this a long time. We aren't helping them by covering up their wrong deeds. It is only getting worse as time goes on. I have to turn them in." A resolution settled over Luka's face like that of which Rose had never seen before.

Completely distraught, Rose jumped to her feet, tears streaming down her pale cheeks. "Luka, I will never forgive you if you do such a thing! These are our brothers you are talking about! Our family, our name! You will only bring us all down. You can't do this!" Rose looked at her friend and the resolution on Luka's face chilled her to the bone. Rose shivered involuntarily; she knew Luka was going to go against her wishes.

"Rose, I must go to the mainland for help! Our community can only handle so much of their evil deeds. You know my grandfather is one of the elders; I have already spoken with him privately and he swears there is nothing that can be done. All Grandfather said was, *"Boys will be boys. Their actions will reveal their hearts and lead them where their hearts want to go. There is nothing the council can do to stop them. We have seen nothing except foolish, childish behavior and it will pass as they grow older. The Council will not interfere until there is proof of wrong-doing."* Rose, the Alaska State Troopers have to be notified about these girls, about our brothers' actions of stealing and boot-legging, or it will never stop! Don't you see? Datka will be filled with illegal alcohol and prostitution! Do you want to see our own little children that you and I will one day have live in this, Rose? Our parents don't *want* to see; the elders in our community are powerless to stop them. Do we want to watch another group of young people go down again, Rose?"

Images flitted before Luka's eyes...*her older brother Henry, who she once idolized, his limp, lifeless body brought to her parents' home. Snatches of words catching her young ears about alcohol, an accident on the choppy waters, his head striking a rock, and another boat of fishermen seeing the accident involving her* *brother and his boat of drunken friends.....*Luka shut her eyes tight to ward off the images.

She gripped Rose's arms tightly between her fingers. "Remember my older brother, Henry. For his sake I can't let Markus or Andrew follow his path to destruction and death. Markus, Andrew, Peter, Joshua....they all have power over our parents and the elders in this community that is unlike before. I have heard the Council talking about the power of this generation of young men and young women, the disrespect for authority, for family, how easy it is for them to buy alcohol, and do whatever they want in Seal Harbor. The ones only a few years older than you and I hate Datka and what it stands for. That is what is destroying everything, Rose! Their numbers are more than the ones before them who destroyed themselves and tried to bring their evil ways to this Island. I can't watch this happen again. We were young girls then, Rose, helpless to do anything, but now we *can* do something to save them, to save us, to save our people. One person can make a difference, Rose. If that one person does something to change a situation. I will do it alone if I have to." Rose had never seen Luka so strong before. She both admired and feared her friend's tenacity and convictions.

Rose shut her eyes tight to try to clear her mind. She opened them again and spoke slowly, quietly to Luka. "Luka, think about what you are saying you will do. How will this affect you? Your family? Me and my family? You will bring only more trouble to the Island if you involve outsiders, the authorities. Let Datka handle their own!" With that, Rose ran off blindly and Luka bowed her head and silently cried tears of regret, knowing she had no other choice, even if it cost Luka the only girl who would ever be her best friend.

*********************

For the third night in a row, Rose lay shivering under the sparse blankets. She was accustomed to several more layers, especially missing her soft, bear hide blanket. But thoughts of a little boy snug under her old blanket made her at least warm inside. Rose knew she had a soft spot for the little ones. She had heard one of the little boys who had lost his home telling his older sister how cold he had been the night before and how much he missed his blanket. The boy's home and all of his family's belongings had been destroyed in the fire. Never farther away than her next breath, Rose felt the deep guilt over her brother being a party to starting the fire. She determined to do whatever she could to help the families in need, even if it meant her discomfort! Rose hoped that maybe the personal discomfort she endured would ease the guilt in her soul over the horrific events. The least she could do was give the little one her warm blanket. She had several more to use at home. But without it, Rose was very aware of how much of a barrier it had created to hold in the heat during the frigid evenings. Gladly though, her little friend was sleeping warmer tonight.

Rose lay there thinking of all of the needs the families had. Pots and pans, eating and cooking utensils, baskets, bedding, clothing, even toys for the younger ones. So many necessities lost. She hadn't even allowed her mind to think about the few keepsakes and family heirlooms that were irreplaceable. Rose's young heart ached for these families and friends. Her mother and aunt had given away anything extra or non-essential to their own homes to help the struggling families. Others had done the same, but the needs were still great.

Another shiver coursed through Rose's body, though she wasn't sure if it was from the cold evening or from the cold condition of her heart. Hate seemed to be finding its way into her soul; its icy fingers slowly but surely wrapping around her thoughts and heart. *How could my brother be so stupid? He has risked so very much just for fun and to impress girls of the night. Why would he act so foolishly? And now, my best friend Luka is acting just as foolishly as the boys have, only her actions are going to be worse! She will utterly destroy my family and hers when she gives out the information she has. No one will respect our fathers and their businesses will suffer dearly. She just needs to keep her mouth shut!*

Again, another shiver. Rose tried to pull the covers around her tighter to ward off the cold. Her bones and heart ached; she wasn't sure which hurt the worst. Finally beginning to drift off to sleep, her last words floating through her mind were, *We need a rescuer, someone to save our island from this tragedy.* Sleep completely consumed Rose; so did her dreams....

*Blue, bluer than the waters around the island. Two hands outstretched towards her. "It's going to be okay. I will help." Fear and curiosity vied for control in her mind. This tall stranger standing before her, towering over her, all glowing and blue, familiar, yet still a stranger. Her hands remained motionless by her side, unable to move to reach for the angel-man's. Behind him she could see things she wanted, needed, but was too afraid to ask for, too afraid to reach out. "Who are you?" Rose asked the stranger. He didn't answer, only stood with hands outstretched. Ever so slightly he began to drift away from her, like he was walking backwards but without moving his blue legs, fading, slowly, slowly, away from her still form.....*

---

"Don't leave! We need you!" Rose startled herself awake as she heard the words come from her mouth. She sat upright, caught in that strange place between sleeping and waking. Rose's thoughts began to tumble one over another. *I have seen him before in my dreams, that same man, the angel-man. Who is he? Why am I haunted by him? Why do we need him? How can a dream-man help?*

Brushing slender fingers through her long hair, Rose quickly dressed. She could no longer sleep, that much she knew. *I need to walk, to get some fresh air. All of this mess lately has my mind in a jumble.* Pulling on fur-lined boots, Rose called Stormy to her side. The malamute was only too eager to walk with Rose. Bending down to bury her face in the dog's soft, warm coat, she felt an unwanted tear slip from her lashes. Stormy licked her face and whimpered at Rose. "Okay, girl, let's go." She headed down the familiar trail and took her time. Stormy would run ahead chasing some scent she had found, on the trail of a fox or other small animal.

Instead of her thoughts clearing from the walk, they began to rush in like the shore's tide. *How can someone I have never met appear in my dreams? He both scares and invites me at the same time. Maybe the rescuer we need on this island? Maybe too much stew for dinner? It's all so confusing.* Rose felt the pull of her household responsibilities and decided to turn back.

She walked towards the house by the back way and passed where her father kept his fishing equipment stored. The shed door was ajar. Rose was afraid an animal would enter it or a small child so she went to shut the door for her father. Before she reached the door, her brother stepped out, arms loaded with fishing poles, nets, equipment that were the tools of their father's trade. She quickly stopped in her tracks and stood motionless so as not to attract her brother's attention. Andrew's head was down and he moved quickly out of the shed, shutting the door with his foot. He ran off down the side trail in the opposite direction, arms loaded, never seeing his sister. When she knew he was far enough away, Rose moved once again. She went to the door of the shed and opened it to peer in. *What is Andrew doing with father's things? Maybe father sent Andrew to gather supplies he needed for the day's catch and bring them to him at the boat.* Rose shut the shed door and headed inside the house.

Hearing her parents stirring inside, she quickly made the coffee and porridge. Rose's mother came to her side and hugged her daughter. "How did you sleep?" Rose started to blurt out the dreams that were recurring and discuss them with her mother but decided against it.

"I slept about like usual. I woke early and went for a walk with Stormy and have just returned. How is father?"

"He had an easier night last evening. Didn't cough as much. I hope today will be good for him. He needs to fish. We need money." Her once beautiful mother was showing signs of stress and hard-work on her small frame. She was still a very attractive woman even at her age. Rose just hated to see the toll these past few weeks had taken on her mother.

"Maybe I can help you weave some extra baskets today. We are getting close to tourism season and the more we weave, the more money we can earn. Two is better than one. Did father send Andrew ahead with the fishing gear? I was hoping Andrew would help father out more." Rose went to the shelf and reached for two cups. She poured herself and her mother each a cup of coffee. When Rose's mother didn't answer, she turned to look at her.

"Did you say your brother left with the fishing gear? That makes no sense. Father has just awakened. I heard Andrew stirring around long before us so I know he wasn't told to get any gear. Are you sure about this?"

A foreboding feeling filled Rose's chest. Not wanting to alarm her parents, she quickly said, "Mother, do not worry. Maybe Andrew decided on his own to fish today since father hasn't felt well lately. I will check it out and see. I am sure that is what has happened. Do not worry father about it. Maybe Andrew intends to surprise him." Rose pasted on a smile and fixed her mother something to eat. "Eat breakfast while it is warm. If you get out the weaving, I will return and help you in a bit." She kissed her mother's forehead and put her coat on again.

Heading down the same path her brother had gone, Rose dreaded what she would find in the minutes ahead.

# CHAPTER 17

After their luggage was collected and a car secured for the Parkers' use, they made the five minute drive to a local Alaskan restaurant. Gabe loved the Alaskan cuisine, especially all of the different selections of fish like salmon, halibut, and crab. Moose meat was another of his favorites. It was quite a switch from his mother's wonderful home cooking. They ordered everything from moose steaks to grilled salmon around the table and engaged in small talk with the Millers while they waited on their food.

So far Gabe had learned some details about the beautiful, intriguing Jade. She was born and raised in Florida, was homeschooled until she graduated, and had been on several short-term mission trips with her parents to Mexico, Honduras, and Guatemala until they had been called to Alaska three years ago. She had taken Spanish all through her high school years hoping it would benefit her on mission trips. Jade was as fluent in speaking Spanish as she was English and would at times lapse easily into Spanish when speaking to her parents. They would quickly remind her that she was in Alaska, not Mexico, which brought a slight blush to her cheeks. Jade enjoyed talking about the mission field as much as the adults. Her conversation was sprinkled with references to her faith and God.

Gabe and Ed both remained mostly silent during the meal as they devoured their wonderful dinners of thick steaks and fresh fish while they listened to the adults and Jade. Unsure if fatigue and hunger had closed their mouths or the young beauty sitting across from them, Gabe decided he must seem impolite or disinterested. Gabe spoke directly to Jade, "What do you like most about missions work?" He looked into her mesmerizing green eyes lined with thick dark lashes while she answered him.

"Gabe?" Jade was asking him a question, had been speaking for he had no idea how long, and he hadn't heard a word she said. Now it was his turn to blush crimson.

Ed flung a quick elbow jab at him that brought Gabe out of his stupor. "Wake up, Gabe! The lady asked you a question."

Gabe quickly coughed to hide his embarrassment. "I'm sorry, Jade. Not enough sleep lately preparing for this trip. Please excuse my rudeness! What did you ask me?"

Jade giggled at Gabe's discomfort. Her hand made it to the cross around her neck, an unconscious move on her part. "I had just given you a run down on what I like most about mission work then asked you to pass the salt."

He quickly reached for the salt shaker and knocked over the steak sauce in the process. Jade giggled again. *So much for impressing the lady,* Gabe huffed silently at himself. He finally grabbed hold of the salt shaker and handed it to her.

"Thanks, Gabe. I didn't mean to present you with such a challenge, *hombre torpe.*" Another giggle.

Having grown up in Texas, Ed knew enough Spanish to know what Jade had said. He busted out laughing and just shook his head at Gabe's unusual clumsiness.

"Okay, that's not fair!" Gabe began laughing with the both of them. "What did she say, Buddy?"

"Don't worry about it, *clumsy man.* The lady could have been much more brutal. While you zoned out on us, Jade was telling us she enjoyed most everything about the mission field especially working with the children. She told about the times they held Vacation Bible Schools in Guatemala for the village children, then she asked you for the salt. Consider yourself caught up now, *hombre torpe.*" Ed laughed at his own humor along with Jade; when they both noticed Gabe wasn't laughing they quickly hid their snickers behind their napkins.

"Thanks a lot." Gabe made a conscious effort to pay attention through the remainder of the meal and to not be distracted by Jade's beauty and personality to the point of being mute or clumsy. He liked a girl with spunk and she obviously had some.

Jade was no dummy. She knew Gabe's distraction wasn't lack of sleep. She also had a hard time focusing with two handsome, charming, Christian men sitting across from her. *It ought to be interesting these next few weeks with two gorgeous guys around constantly.* To keep her focus, she decided to carry the conversation. Jade turned to Gabe. "What has your experience been like on the mission field, Gabe?" Her jade-green eyes shone with complete attentiveness.

"I've been around mission work since I could walk, so that's a loaded question. In a nut shell, the Aleutians are like another family to me. I love Alaska and the people, third only to God and my own family. I haven't been back in around three years because of getting my Associates Degree in Logistics, so I'm really anxious to see them. I guess to quickly sum it up, my heart's desire is to take the gospel and the love of Christ to people who haven't heard of Him yet. My life's passion is to follow God where He leads." The intensity in Gabe's face and words was easily noticeable.

Admiration shined brightly in her eyes as Gabe told his story. "Wow, I'm impressed! I like your heart. I think we will be really good friends, Gabe."

Gabe liked the girl's admiration, something he was unaccustomed to from young ladies. Usually they laughed at him and his love for God and the Aleutian Indians or just couldn't relate to him and mission work.

Jade turned to Ed next. "So, Ed. I can tell you aren't from Washington by your very southern, charming accent. Where did you start serving on the mission field as a young boy?"

Ed's half-grin appeared. "Little lady, I knew nothing of God until about four years ago. This guy next to me had a run-in with me when I was drunk and lost. He took me for coffee and over a pot of java I learned about God, His Son, love, and forgiveness. I found freedom from alcohol not so very long ago, thank you God! I'm not where my buddy is in his walk with Christ, but at least I'm on the same path. The Parkers sort of adopted me as one of their own and I have tagged along on a couple of mission trips before with them and love it. So now I'm hooked."

Gabe noticed Jade's smile slowly fade while Ed talked. When Ed told his testimony, even a brief version, he was oblivious to anything except for the love and grace and mercy God had shown him; he had no idea of Jade's negative reaction. Ed totally missed her smile slip away, the crease in her brow, her body language, the smugness that Gabe witnessed.

Gabe quickly, but nicely, argued Ed's point. "Bro, four years or fourteen years with Christ doesn't matter. It is the heart change, the change of course that is important."

Jade faced Gabe again, her beautiful smile back in place. "Gabe, fourteen years with Christ gives a person much more Christian experience, more wisdom, and obviously they are closer to God than someone who's only been with Him for just a few years."

Ed frowned, pondering her statement as he pushed the remains of his salad around on his plate. "I haven't thought of that, Jade. I guess I've got a long way to go then." A slight sadness caused Ed's shoulders to slump.

Gabe opened his mouth to dispute Jade's statement but didn't get the chance. Jim stood from the table and said, "I know you all are tired. Let's head out and get you settled for the evening."

Gabe made a mental note to re-visit this topic as soon as the opportunity arose.

The evening came to a close as the Millers helped their newly arrived friends get settled in their rooms at the AMRA headquarters. Knowing tomorrow they would each need to hit the ground running, Rand and Becca, Gabe, and Ed all fell fast asleep as soon as their exhausted heads hit the pillows.

# CHAPTER 18

Andrew couldn't get an image out of his mind. It chased him down relentlessly; no matter how much he made his legs hurry up, the image kept up with him as well. As vivid as the day he saw it happen, he could see the chase…..the beautiful, thick-furred wolf, the small, quick hare, one chasing the other for a meal, to satisfy its gnawing hunger, the other just trying to stay alive and escape the terrors of the wolf's claws and jaws.

Andrew felt like both the hunter and the hunted. The scary thing was both were vying for attention inside his soul. He needed to hunt, and at the same time, was being hunted. But his driving force wasn't a meal; instead it was a bottle. He *needed* and *wanted* liquor so badly he was willing to do whatever it took to get it, thus the hunt. He was chasing down any means for money to make his purchase. But on the other side of this chase was the little hare just trying to survive, to stay out of harm's way, to run fast enough, to dart quickly enough to stay out of the wolf's deadly reach. His soul felt like the hare, small, defenseless, out of breath and out of hiding places. On the run from being caught stealing, on the run from this new addiction, these new pleasures that once delighted him but now were doing him in. On the run from the very ones he had once loved more than life, but now was willing to use to feed his unending desire.

Andrew couldn't believe how far he had slipped, a slow, almost imperceptible slip at first, but gradually it had picked up speed and become a downward, slippery, unstoppable slide. Like the time he was standing at the top of an icy hill. He hadn't realized ice covered the other side of the hill until it was too late. He lost his footing, just sliding at first when he headed down the other side on a sheet of ice. By then it was too late to do much about it. The downward slant of the icy hillside created just enough momentum to cause his slippery descent to pick up speed and land him at the bottom only inches away from a tree. The thing Andrew knew now was that he was in the process of gaining momentum down this slippery hill of deceit, with no way of stopping, nothing to grab hold of to stop his out of control descent. Would there be a large unmovable tree at the bottom for him to crash into? He couldn't see what was at the bottom of this scary, tumultuous hill. But he knew down deep that a crash was inevitable.

Guilt was on his heels constantly chasing and biting at him. *Was all of this worth it? This freedom, the alcohol, the girls? Was stealing and causing a fire on the Island and lying and hiding all worth the guilt and turmoil he was feeling today?* Andrew simply could not out-run the guilt that was relentless. It was wearing him down.

Not an hour went by that he didn't recall the stupid mistake he had made, all for a girl's attention. He had not meant to start the fire. He only wanted to scare the girls, which in turn sent them scurrying like scared rabbits into the guys' arms. One minute they all were sitting around the small bonfire with Peter telling another one of his terrifying, bone-chilling tales of the Shaman, the Aleut Medicine Man, who haunted young girls at night looking for locks of their hair for his medicinal use. The next minute Andrew had discreetly picked up a dry piece of wood and tossed it into the fire hoping to scare the girls.

The wood sent sparks up into the trees above and into the dry sedges surrounding them. Before any of them knew what was happening, the low bushes were aflame and spreading quickly due to the dry conditions in the past month. Fire was headed straight for the closely built homes! And all they did was run away afraid. Guilt, now his closest companion was about to bring him down.

Continuing down the path in front of him, he was beginning to feel the weight of the items he had taken from his father's fishing shed. Not only the physical weight of his load, but the weight on his heart and mind.

Stealing had never been something he had done before. One time had now turned into a dozen times. Andrew and his cousin Joshua had become quite good at stealing, as long as they were sober when they took things from their neighbors and family. Andrew didn't let himself think about whom he was stealing from, only he focused on the outcome of selling the items in Seal Harbor and what he could purchase in the end.

The liquor and girls had become the driving force behind his actions. Surely no one would notice all of the little things they had taken over the course of the last several months. But having to figure out what to do about his father's things being gone was an entirely different matter. The girls were demanding more money than they were at first so he had to sell more things, not just trinkets, but things that brought a higher price. So with his father's stolen things, Andrew was headed toward the boat and into Seal Harbor where a buyer who didn't ask questions could always be found.

About half way down the trail to the shoreline, Andrew heard the sound of alert he and his friends had devised, the bird call of a ptarmigan. He froze in place, listening. Immediately Peter stepped out of the low-standing bushes.

"Peter, you about scared me to death! Why did you make the bird call? What is wrong?" Andrew fought to calm his racing heart. What he was about to do was making his heart race fast enough; now this.

Peter shoved Andrew into a more secluded place off the trail's path causing Andrew to drop a couple of things from his dad's gear. He bent to quickly retrieve them knowing he needed all the money he could get and wasn't going to sacrifice a thing. Peter grabbed him roughly by the arm and hissed in Andrew's ear, "Shut up, you fool! Do you want to get us caught?"

Fear made Andrew stop and listen to what Peter had to say and look around cautiously, hoping he hadn't been followed. Seeing no one, his heart calmed some. Listening intently to Peter, Andrew felt the words he heard chill him to the bone, striking fear in his heart like never before.

********************

After Peter left, Andrew continued down the way he had started five minutes before. Reaching his father's boat, Andrew quickly loaded the stolen goods and grabbed the oars. With the winds blowing hard this morning he would make it to Seal Harbor in less than two hours. With every slash of the oars through the icy waters, thoughts slashed through Andrew's mind as steadily as the stroke of his oars. As if the wind were on his side, his little boat was being helped along to Seal Harbor to the desires and way of life that held such intrigue and adventure for the searching 20 year old. Thoughts churning like the waters, Andrew couldn't stop his mind from wandering if he had wanted to.

*This fishing equipment should yield a high price. Peter knows of a man who will pay me well. Father will never know I took his things. There are too many desperate families on Datka right now; I can find several to cast the blame on. They need money too, so surely Father will believe one of them could be the thief and not me. Anyway, Father will never blame me for this and I can get what I want – another step closer to moving from that desolate island.*

For one quick moment, guilt and shame overshadowed Andrew's desires. *How could I steal from my own innocent father?* But immediately the lure of his destination overcame his guilty conscience. Andrew continued rowing, faster, harder.

*Father cannot survive this wretched sickness much longer. Soon all of this will be mine anyway to do with as I choose. I'll never fish or trap a day in my life! I won't be tied down to Datka! I have greater plans for myself than that, and Seal Harbor is just the place I want to be. Girls, liquor, money, adventure, opportunities!*

*Peter is already living his dream. His father doesn't expect him to sell his soul to Datka and to fishing. Why can't Father understand that I don't want to inherit his trade and live like he does?*

Andrew thought back to the first trip to Seal Harbor he had taken alone. Being sent on an errand by his sick father, Andrew felt like he was being sent across the ocean to discover a new world. Always before, he traveled with Father to order or pick up supplies or to sell furs, dried salmon, and his mother's handmade clothes and baskets to the shop owners who depended on the Aleutian Indians to keep them in business. Father always had their specific route planned. No matter how much pleading Andrew would do to try to persuade his Father to let him go into certain parts of town, he refused. Father always told him that evil lived in parts of Seal Harbor, evils that Andrew didn't need to find. Andrew wasn't allowed to venture off on his own. Eventually when Father tired quickly, he was forced to sit for a while and send Andrew with the remainder of the errands and money to finish his purchases. Andrew quickly did his father's bidding wanting to prove he could handle the tasks.

In the last year when Father couldn't leave home to fish or trap except sporadically, he definitely couldn't make the windy trip to Seal Harbor. He began by allowing Andrew to take the boat for several small errands then later, by force of necessity, sent him alone to sell their goods. Andrew loved these trips; he felt free and in charge.

One trip in particular would always stick in his mind. He had a load of furs and baskets to unload and sell. Andrew had plans to take a walk into the center of town after selling their goods and just see for himself what he was missing and if Peter's stories of town were accurate. Quickly docking the boat, Andrew began to unload the baskets and heavy furs. Intent on his work, he heaved the last pile onto the shop owner's waiting cart.

Turning, he noticed a young girl, probably close to his age, leaning on the dock rail about twenty feet from him watching him work. Andrew took a quick glance around and saw no one but himself on the dock. Unaccustomed to this attention, he gave her a little smile and turned back to the cart. Lifting the handles and pushing with all his might, he started it rolling down the dock.

When Andrew got close to her she took two steps in his direction and paused. He stopped the cart and heard her quietly say, "I know where you sell your furs. When you are done, you can find me two streets over to the north." With a little wave she slowly walked before Andrew and towards the street she had directed him to.

Not able to keep his eyes off her pretty form, Andrew took hold of the cart once again and determined to quickly finish his sells. Interest, excitement, uncertainty all vied for position in his mind. *Why not? This is why I am here, to see what Seal Harbor has for me.*

Finishing with the shop owner and pocketing the money, Andrew returned the now empty cart to the back of the shop. He looked towards the street where the girl had directed him to meet her and saw a figure give a little wave in his direction. She had been watching him the whole time he was finishing his business. Andrew made eye contact with her and followed her lead towards a small run-down porch attached to a building in need of repair. She stepped up to the porch and turned back to see if Andrew was still following her.

Noise and music filled the air around him as he approached the building. *This must be one of the bars that Peter is always talking about.* Apprehension slowed his steps. Andrew knew he was under the legal age by one year to purchase alcohol. Plus he didn't have any money of his own.

Seeing him pause, the girl walked over to the porch rail and leaned over. "What's the matter? Scared?"

He could see teasing in her eyes. Andrew hated to be mocked or teased. "No, just in a hurry. What's your name?"

Andrew fought to seem in control and calm though his gut was churning.

"Berta. What's yours, handsome?" She batted long eyelashes at him and held out a delicate hand.

Andrew reached for her small hand and said with shaking voice, "An-Andrew." Quickly he withdrew his hand and cleared his throat.

Berta giggled at him which caused his cheeks to redden, another thing he hated doing. "Well, good to meet you Berta. Good-bye." Turning on his heel, Andrew took off down the street as quickly as he could. *Ugh! She will think I am such a child,* he chided himself.

Andrew headed back towards the boat and forgot his earlier planned trip into town. He finished his father's errands and headed back to Datka angry that a girl could distract him completely and ruin his plans.

A few days later when he saw Peter, he asked if Peter knew of a girl named Berta. After Andrew's description of her, Peter laughed at him for leaving such a girl behind. Berta was known around Peter's part of town for being available to a man for the small price of a bottle of liquor and a meal, such a small price to pay for such a beauty. A price that would later cost Andrew more than he could pay.

It only took several more trips to Seal Harbor for Andrew to overcome his trepidation and to find the courage to talk to Berta. Andrew learned from her that she and a few of her friends were just looking for some boys to have fun with.

One day when she actually talked him into entering the building she had originally lead him to, there in the pool hall surrounded by men and women near his own age, Andrew was exposed to a world that he didn't even know existed, Peter's world. At twenty, Andrew was a year too young to buy alcohol, but in this pool hall, age wasn't important to the owner, only how much liquor he could sell. Andrew met Berta's friends and found out the girls really didn't require much to have a good time; a meal and a bottle of booze was all they wanted from the boys.

Peter knew of an abandoned house on Datka that he had used often. The first few times they brought the girls to an old house nearer to the village, but fearing they would be discovered, Peter began taking them to one that was almost to the other side of the Island away from the village; this became their own private little world. Peter began to arrange for him or Andrew to pick up four of the girls and bring them back to Datka under the cover of night to spend a day or two with him, Andrew, Joshua, and Markus in their secret, abandoned house.

At first the girls only asked for food and booze; lately, they required more from the boys to come to the island with them. Now they wanted money for their "time." The first time Andrew gave Berta money, he felt so sick at his stomach that he had to leave their hide out for a moment to vomit up his meager meal. Reality hit him square in his gut; he was paying a girl to do his bidding, to sleep with him. He was paying for this kind of life, this world of Peter's that he had wanted so badly, a world that had suddenly made him sick. But not sick enough to turn away.

# CHAPTER 19

Running back as fast as she could on her snow shoes, Luka knew she had found a few more pieces to the puzzle. Her week of spying and sneaking around was turning up things she hadn't wanted to find but knew she must discover. Since the day she and Rose had seen the boys and girls in the house near the village, she was on a quest to know what they were up to. Something inside Luka screamed at her to pursue this. Her people were at risk. Her village where she would one day raise a family of her own was now being threatened by young men she knew and loved. They didn't foresee this, but Luka could. The loss of her older brother who had headed down the same path that her younger brother was now taking was overwhelming at times, almost crippling to Luka, but at the same time giving her the energy and strength to carry on down a path that she knew would be nothing but evil.

Luka had continued to watch daily for the boys to meet at the abandoned house near the village, but after no one had shown up and she knew the boys had gone to Seal Harbor, Luka decided to go have another look inside. Terrified more than she had ever felt in her life, Luka sat as still as a mouse and watched the house to make sure no one was coming. She quickly, quietly crept inside and looked around. Enough daylight came through the broken windows for her to see. Empty bottles littered the floors; broken, old furniture and discarded trash from food was lying around just as she had last seen when she and Rose had looked in the windows. Hoping to discover what the boys were up to, she found nothing of use in the house to give her any clue.

Now after a half-day's time spent looking for the boys' new hide-out, things began falling into place for Luka and her discoveries.  Last night when Markus was home, she overheard a conversation between him and Joshua that lead her directly to their new hideout.  Early this morning she set out to find it and within two hours, she had discovered it. Obviously the boys and girls were now meeting here.  There were fresh footprints, trash, bottles and other apparent clues to them being here.  Both relief at finding the place and disgust at her findings consumed her for a moment.  Luka now knew where to tell the authorities to find them.

Not able to get far enough away fast enough, Luka continued to run toward what was familiar to her.  She now needed the comfort and security of home, of the village.

Without warning she fell flat on her face, the wind knocked from her already burning lungs.  Gasping for air, Luka felt the weight of someone lying on top of her back, pinning her face to the ground.

Before she could react, a hand covered her mouth and flipped her over onto her back. Staring into the blackest eyes Luka had ever seen, she couldn't tell anything about who had slammed her to the ground. The face was covered with a hood with only eye and mouth-holes cut away.

Something sharp and shiny appeared before her eyes and was pressed to her neck. She caught a glimpse of an elk antler-handled knife and felt the blade pressing into her throat, bringing fear that almost caused her to pass out.

Words were being hissed close to her face, words laced with liquor-scented breath. "Unless you want to die, stay away. I will kill you if I ever see you on this side of the Island again! You don't know what you are getting into. Never come near here again. Stay in your little village with your mouth closed or I will shut it permanently. Do you understand me, girl?"

The knife pressed harder onto Luka's windpipe, making her see spots dance before her eyes. Unable to speak, she nodded her head as much as she could. The figure took the tip of his knife and drew it down the side of her cheek just enough to draw a trickle of blood.

"Now get up and run as fast away from here as you can before I change my mind and kill you like I would a small hare."

Without looking back, Luka struggled to her feet and ran as fast as her snow shoes would allow towards the village. Nearing the village, Luka found a huge boulder and hid behind it. Trembling from head to toe, she fought with all her might to calm her racing heart. Fear gripped her like a trap on a helpless animal's leg.

Luka wiped at her cheek. It wasn't bleeding now but she could feel the dried blood and swollen streak on her face. She would just have to tell her parents that a tree limb struck her in the face and cut her. No one could know what had just happened. No one, not even Rose.

Burying her face in her mittened hands, Luka did something she hadn't done since she was a little girl; she prayed. *God above, You saved me, I know it. Please calm my heart. Help me, for I am so afraid. That man could have killed me, of that I am sure. I don't know what to do. Please show me.*

Almost instantly, like a gentle breeze, peace settled over Luka. She knew it was God; the experience she had just endured with the unknown man should leave her quaking for days and right now, she felt peace.

Luka knew she wasn't alone, that God was with her even now. Quietly, softly, she heard words that lit a tiny flame of hope in her. *Speak the truth in love. I am with you.*

Little did the stranger know, his threat only strengthened her resolve, for it had pushed her to a place she hadn't been to in years, since the missionaries had come to Datka last, to the arms of God. Luka knew what she had to do, only today she was assured she would not be alone.

# CHAPTER 20

Alaska Missionaries Relief Aid headquarters was buzzing with activity. Preparations were already underway for the Aleutian families on Datka Island. The needs were great, but the relief team knew what they were doing. John Miller and Gabriel Parker made a great pair; John could see the needs that needed to be met and had valuable resources and contacts already in place for AMRA'S use, and Gabe could organize gathering the supplies, arranging the bush planes they would need, and scheduling the trips to and from Datka. Becca, Jade, and Jill were also great assets to Gabe and John because they could foresee the practical, household items the people would need. Gabe had turned the entire construction projects for the homes and school repairs over to Ed and Randall. Things were falling into place beautifully for the team. With only two days before flying to the Island, each knew there was not a second to be wasted.

Every trip to Datka served its own unique purpose. Rand and Becca had been on many, each one as special and memorable as the other. Rand thought back to his and Becca's conversation as they lay in bed the evening before. Both had felt that this trip would be different, more than just to bring relief to their friends on Datka Island. Neither could identify what the difference would be, but each knew God had greater things in mind for all of them involved.

They lay in each other's arms reminiscing of trips in their past. Becca giggled as she remembered their first trip as young newly-weds and how she hadn't packed sufficient enough clothing for either of them. Their warm, Washington, winter clothing was not even close to what they needed in the windy, rainy, freezing temperatures of Datka. By day two of their first trip, their missionary leader and new Aleutian Indian family had come up with enough extra clothing for them. The pictures from this trip still made Becca laugh. She and Rand looked like two overstuffed, fur-trimmed sausages. On all other trips since then, they took coats, long underwear, boots, and any other polar-winter wear they could buy.

On another trip, pneumonia had begun to spread throughout the old and young on the Island. Their main goal for this trip was to take much needed medicine for the people. Becca's heart broke as she remembered her time being spent with the elderly as they passed from this world into the next. All she could do was bring a little comfort to the dying in their last moments and mourn with those left behind. There were two occasions on that trip that she and Rand were able to lead two precious souls to come to know Jesus as their Lord and Savior before they left their earthly bodies. Rand and Becca watched several of the little ones, who would have died without the medicine they brought, recover before their trip back home. The joy in the parents' eyes in seeing their babies survive was enough to make that difficult trip worth it.

On every mission trip their goal was to teach the people about God, their Creator, and His Son, Jesus, who made them, loved them, died for them, and wanted them to live free, peaceful lives. So many of the Aleutians struggled with alcoholism and depression. They needed what Rand and Becca had, a real, deep, enduring relationship with God and His Son. This couple knew they could offer hope and a better life for their friends. Early on, both Rand and Becca struggled with wanting to *change* the Aleutians, to make life easier for them, to teach them different ways to provide for their families. But quickly they learned of something much more solid, more foundationally important in the Aleutians: their sense of family, community, honor, and hard-work. The Parkers had never seen such a fierceness and determination than in their Alaskan friends. The Aleutians were able and willing to provide for their families, to work harder than anyone Rand and Becca had ever met even though conditions were far from easy. "Americanizing" the Aleutians wasn't what they needed; God's love and a helping hand was. Not outsiders to come in and change them, but to support them. And that is what shaped the Parkers' future trips to Datka.

After Gabe was born and old enough to travel with Rand and Becca for short-term trips, their goal became spreading the gospel and telling the people of God's love. Every trip they made, they held Vacation Bible School for the children. Becca had the mothers work right by her side with the children, knowing she needed their help and that they would also hear the gospel. The children loved Gabe and his fair skin and blond hair. He loved their darker skin and black hair and easy smiles. Gabe played games with them from sun-up to sun-down when the children weren't busy helping their parents or attending VBS classes. They were little sponges, soaking up the love of God and the Bible verses Becca taught them. Every return trip she was amazed at the verses and stories from the Bible that she had taught them years before that the little ones could still recall. Each year she added new ones, building upon what they had already learned.

While Becca and young Gabe worked with the children, Rand spent countless hours helping the men repair boats, building new homes or repairing existing ones, and working on the new, larger school building. When Gabe became older, he spent half his time with the young children and the other half working with his dad and the Aleutian men on projects. Rand took the opportunity while he worked closely with the men to tell them of God's love and the gospel. They forged strong relationships through hard work and shared experiences.

Both Rand and Becca were excited to see their old friends, to meet the new babies that had been born in their absence, to see how the children had grown into young men and women. So much changed in one year's time, and this year held many changes for them to discover.

With the morning almost half over, the team wrapped up their meeting with everyone assigned certain jobs. This morning the ladies would finish packing the boxes of household goods and clothing. They also had the job of packing enough food for the mission team for the two week stay on the Island. Never wanting to burden the Aleutians, the missionaries took their own food with them. They contributed to the meals they shared with their Datka friends and made sure they left extra food with them when the missionaries left the Island.

Becca, Jill, and Jade were in a room off to themselves surrounded with empty boxes, clothing, non-perishable food, bedding, cooking utensils, pots, pans, toys, and many other assorted items to ease the needs on the Island. Conversation flowed easily among the three women. Becca and Jill became fast friends, finding they had many things in common, from a love for Alaska and its native people, to mission work, to a love for cooking and raising their families, and reading richly-plotted novels.

Becca wanted to get to know Jade better, especially since her son would be working closely with Jade over the next few months. She began by asking Jade questions about herself. "So, Jade. Tell me a little about yourself. I know you are twenty years old, were raised in Florida, have been home-schooled, been on several mission trips....What are some of your goals and dreams at this stage in life?"

Jade flipped her dark hair over her shoulder, fiddled with her necklace, and looked at Becca. Her green eyes lit up at the question. "Well....I know I want to continue in the mission field, like my parents have. I love meeting new people and having new adventures. One day I would like to meet a man who has the same goals as I do, travel, do mission work together, have wonderful adventures, raise a family later on. I want to meet someone on the same level as me in my walk with God. Someone as close to Him as I am, a man that has lived a, hmmm.....spotless, pure life, like me, a virgin, Christ-centered, mature. That all may sound a bit selfish, but I know what I do and don't want in life and in a future mate."

Becca noticed Jill's slight frown. Jill remained silent during her daughter's answer, but Becca could see that Jill's body language displayed her displeasure.

In her sweet way, Becca responded to Jade. "Wow, you do seem to know what you want out of life. That may be a bit hard to find a young man like that though. *Spotless* isn't everything, Jade. If you meet a man who maybe had lived a life that wasn't full of the best choices and later, he found Christ, he would still be as *spotless*, as you say, as the one who had lived a life of excellent, purer choices. You know as well as I do, Jade, that when a person comes to know Christ, He forgives their sin and makes them white as snow, even someone with a soiled past."

Jade was quick to respond to Becca. "I understand, Mrs. Becca, but I really think someone on my level, like me, would make me happier. There would be a lot less relational issues to deal with than if I met a man who had lived a careless, wild life before Christ. That's very high on my list. It would make us more compatible."

"Maybe so. Just don't overlook all of the wonderful guys out there that do have a different past than you, that now have chosen to live for Christ and not themselves any longer. It's really all about their hearts more than their past, honey."

"I hear you, Mrs. Becca. But I believe I can have both if I'm patient. I'd better let Gabe know we are done with these boxes. I'm sure there will be more for us to do." She gave Becca a quick hug as she left the two women.

When Jade left, Jill quietly turned to Becca. "I'm so sorry about my daughter's attitude. She is such a sweet girl, but very confident. She sounds so self-seeking even to her own mother. I don't know how to handle these ideas of hers. It's not something John and I agree with completely. We purposely raised her in church, to know God, and to think of others first. But lately, she seems fixated on a perfect future and a perfect mate that I am afraid just doesn't exist. I'm afraid the decision to home-school and shelter Jade maybe has given her a view of life that is unrealistic. John and I are both troubled by this."

Becca walked over to Jill and put an arm around her new friend's shoulder. "Don't throw in the towel just yet. Home-schooling has its benefits. Parents seem to believe they can shelter their children from all of the evil in the world, but it's just not possible. Randall and I are public school teachers. We see all kinds of evil, but light outshines the darkness and we have been called to be light in our school. At times, I wanted to home-school Gabe or put him in private school, so I know the decision to home-school Jade wasn't made lightly.

I'm sure you and John had your reasons. But like Rand and I have found with Gabe, all children reach a point that their faith and beliefs and morals must become their *own*. Not just because we raised them to believe or act a certain way, but because it goes deeper into the core of their own hearts. Jade will have to now decide exactly what she believes, what truths she embraces, what is in her young heart that she will make as her own. You and John just keep praying for her sweet heart. She's in that season of decision-making, of claiming and making what she believes and wants her own. And as parents, it's difficult to hear what comes out of their mouths at times when they are in this season."

Jill sighed deeply and a small smile crossed her face. "Thank you, Becca. I needed that." Jill gave Becca a hug and swiped at a stray tear. "Ok, let's tackle the next project."

# CHAPTER 21

Gabe looked up from his desk as the dark-haired, green-eyed beauty walked into his office. She took his breath away each time he saw her. *Focus, man,* he reminded himself. To Jade, he said, "What can I do for you, Jade?"

She flashed a grin at Gabe. "I just wanted to report to the leader that the women have now packed all of the boxes and we await our next assignment." She gave him a mock salute then giggled at her silliness.

Gabe laughed with Jade. He quickly put on a mock-serious expression. "Well, it seems I put three capable women in charge of a huge project and it got completed hours before schedule. Well done, sir...I mean, ma'am." Gabe grinned, enjoying their joking with each other. He found himself quickly lost in her green eyes for the moment.

Jade blushed at his admiration of her and the work that had been accomplished. "So, can I help you with something, Gabe?" she sweetly asked.

"Actually, yes. I need some ideas on the Vacation Bible School activities and I could use someone to brainstorm that with me....what kinds of games to play, art projects to do, all of the items we need to take to the island to make VBS a success." He was back in his mode of planning, his focus redirected.

"Perfect. I love working with the children, so I should have some ideas." Her eyes lit up at the thought of working with Gabe for the next couple of hours on a project.

Hearing footsteps, both turned to see Ed enter the office. When he saw Jade, Ed slowed and half-grinned at her unexpected presence. "Hi, Gabe. Howdy, Miss Jade." Jade smiled in his direction but said nothing in return.

"Ed, what's up?" Gabe asked his friend.

"I came to see if you could help me with something, but since Jade's here I may need her instead. John and I are working on the school's construction plans and we both thought we needed another opinion on some things. A female voice might be just what we need to give us some insight. And here's Jade." Turning to her, he asked, "Can I borrow you a minute?"

Not wanting to give up her spot to help Gabe, she said, "Ed, the women and I just finished the boxes so mom and Mrs. Becca will be available. Maybe one of them would be better help to you and dad."

Trying not to look disappointed, Ed said, "Oh, ok. Thanks, ma'am." He nodded his head in her direction.

Jade giggled. "No problem, *Tex*."

"Tex?" Ed questioned.

Jade looked at Ed. "Yeah, I think it's very fitting. You ooze Texas charm with all of your *howdy's* and *ma'am's*. It's perfect for you."

Gabe smirked and said, "See ya later, Tex."

A very red-faced Ed left the office in search of the women.

Gabe busted out laughing. "Now that was funny! Ed isn't usually rendered speechless. You seem to have that affect on him. I think he's smitten with you, ma'am." Gabe laughed at himself and quit when he saw he was the only one laughing. "I'm sorry, Jade. That was uncalled for. I've just never seen my buddy like this before."

"Look. Ed's nice and funny and good-looking and we all enjoy his company, but he's definitely not my type. I'm sure he will be an asset to the team." Her smile quickly returned. "So where were we? VBS plans?"

Dumb-founded, Gabe retorted, "Huh. You're the first girl I've ever heard say that about Ed. He usually has to fight the ladies off. Not your type?" Gabe pressed.

"You know, wild past, not great choices throughout his life, not pure, for lack of a better word, not on the same level as I am. You, Gabe, of all people, know what I mean." His change in expression caused her to stop short. Jade cleared her throat delicately to hide her discomfort at the sound of her own words directed at his best friend. "He's not like you at all, Gabe," she purred.

Gabe's jaw clenched at her words, but he decided to hear her out before responding. "That's one thing you do have right. Ed's not at all like me. I wish I had half the character and heart he does for people. I tend to get caught up in the little things and miss what's really important." He paused, then stood from his desk. "I think the VBS plans can wait for now. There's something else I need to take care of first."

Taking the cue that she was being dismissed, Jade stood and left dumb-founded, without a word.

*How can a girl so beautiful make me so angry?* Gabe thought to himself. Grabbing his running shoes, he knew he needed to head outside for a jog and some fresh air.

# CHAPTER 22

Life had righted itself in the past three hours for Andrew. He had his bottle in one hand and his girl by his side. A few more sips and the nagging, annoying hint of guilt would be gone. His father's stolen things were being put to good use, in his opinion. *All those long days of fishing should bring me rewards. Today, I'm getting mine.* Andrew smiled and took a few more pulls on the bottle.

Berta sank down by Andrew and whispered something in his ear. "Don't worry, Berta. At tonight's poker game when all our friends are here, I'll win us a big pile of money. Then you'll get your share. The next two days and nights are all ours. You can eat, drink, rest, and spend time with me til your heart's content."

With gleaming eyes and a small smile touching her red painted lips, Berta kissed Andrew. He ignored the uneasiness he felt when she got that look on her face. She was here with him because she *wanted* to be, not just for the money.

He heard a noise outside the old house and got up to look out the cracked, hazy window. Andrew saw Markus, Peter, and Joshua with their three girls in tow headed to the house. From the sounds of the girls' giggling and his friends' loud laughter, Andrew knew their party had begun hours earlier.

Stumbling and crashing through the front door, the room filled with raucous laughter, liquor, and those he called his friends. Andrew sighed with contentment. *The next two days will be great. No work, no coughing, old man or nagging mother or nosy sister. Just me, my girl, and my friends.* Andrew leaned his head back against the old, dirty couch and closed his eyes.

Peter roused Andrew from his contented stupor with a small kick to his boot. "Help me bring in the gear and food from the sled."

Andrew knew better than to challenge Peter, but he did anyway. "Get one of the other guys to help you. I just got settled."

Before he knew what was happening, Peter had him by the front of his shirt, up on his feet. Through gritted teeth, Peter said, "I want *you* to help me, Andrew." Peter got the results he wanted with Andrew following him through the door outside.

As soon as the two had reached the sled, Andrew scowled at Peter. "Calm down, Peter. What's gotten into you?"

Peter glowered at Andrew. "Your buddy's sister, that's what! I found her snooping around where she doesn't belong. She was on our side of the island nosing around the place. But trust me, she won't be back again." The evil smile that crossed Peter's face made the hair stand up on the back of Andrew's neck.

Afraid to ask, Andrew said, "What do you mean? You saw Luka here? I'm sure she didn't mean any harm, just got lost or something." Andrew and Markus had always thought of each other's sisters much like their own. He may not have liked the two girls much but they were still family to him, and Andrew or Markus didn't approve of anyone messing with the girls.

With a wicked gleam in his eyes, Peter said, "Trust me, she won't be back around ever again. She knows what is at stake if she returns snooping around here."

Anger flashed across Andrew's face. "What did you do to her?" He knew the depths of evil in his friend and was immediately scared for Luka.

"Shut up, you fool! If I didn't scare her away for good, you and your little Berta would have no place to go now would you?" Peter's face was inches from Andrew's. "I told you I don't like anyone around my place without my permission. Especially a girl that will squeal on us. Let's just say she bears the mark of my reminder." With an evil laugh, Peter retorted, "You will be smart to tell your own sister to stay away from us." With that, Peter spat on the ground and stomped back towards the house leaving Andrew to carry the remainder of the things in from the sled.

Fear gripped his heart. Andrew knew what Peter was capable of. *He better not have hurt Luka. I have to tell her to stay away and warn Rose the next time I see them. He will kill them both if they cross his path again.*

Depositing the things from the sled, Andrew headed straight towards his waiting bottle to find relief from the torment and fear wrestling in his mind. He looked up to see Markus eyeing him from across the room. Quickly turning away unable to bear Markus's stare, Andrew sank lower into the dusty cushions of the couch to escape this new sense of guilt over the girls. *What have Markus and I done? Will our sisters pay for our ways?* Now unable to escape these thoughts, he knew without a doubt that his next two days would be ruined by the threat made to Luka, the thoughts of *what* Peter did to her, the unending guilt of so much, too much, breathing its hot breath in his face.

# CHAPTER 23

Rose awoke in the morning feeling like she was walking on air. Her Uncle James had returned from a trip from Seal Harbor the evening before with the best news she had heard in a long time. She had to find Luka and tell her. With the morning chores behind her, she took off at a dead run to Luka's house. Rose couldn't wait to spread the news to her friends and others in the village. They would all be as elated as she was.

Rose reached Luka's home and saw Luka's mother, Martha at the front of their house talking to Ola and Lydia. Lydia's aged mother, Ola, her husband, Michael, and daughter, Lillian had moved in with Yuri after the fire, a single man who had lost his own mother and sister years ago. Martha and Ola had been friends for many years. The two were enjoying living so close to each other for the time being. Martha, Ola, and Lydia's faces were lit with excitement, each one hugging and laughing and talking all at once.

Rose smiled at the three ladies. "Good morning! You look very happy! Why all of the excitement?" Rose suspected the ladies already had heard the news she had to share.

Martha grabbed Rose's hands in her own. "Oh, Rose! Have you heard? Tomorrow the missionaries will arrive to help us! Your Aunt Aggie came this morning to tell us the news."

Rose smiled at Martha's excitement. "Yes, Martha, I came to see if you had heard about this wonderful news, but I see you have. Is Luka around?"

Martha frowned slightly. "No, Rose. She rose early this morning, did her chores, and headed out the door before I even saw her. I'm not sure what she was doing. You know Luka. She loves to be outside."

"Thank you, Martha. I probably know where to find her. Good-bye, ladies." Rose headed down the familiar path she and Luka often took together towards their favorite secluded spot in search of her friend.

Nearing the huge rock they often met at, Rose heard soft sobbing. She quickened her pace and immediately found her friend crouched on the ground with her face in her hands quietly crying. Rose fell to her knees on the ground beside Luka. "Luka, whatever is wrong? Why are you out here alone crying?"

Luka wouldn't look up at Rose and continued crying. Pulling Luka's hands free from her friend's face, Rose pushed Luka's chin up to look her in the eye. Rose gasped as she saw the long red mark on Luka's cheek. "Luka, what happened to your face? Are you ok?"

Luka finally made eye contact with Rose. She wouldn't answer her friend. Fear filled her eyes as she stayed quiet.

"Luka, you are scaring me! Tell me what happened!" Rose took Luka in her arms and hugged her close to quiet her crying.

Finally Luka was able to speak. "Oh, Rose. I don't even want to speak of it. But if I don't, I am afraid you will be hurt too. Two nights ago I overheard Markus and Peter talking and they mentioned their new hide-out. I knew they had abandoned the old house close to the village but had no clue as to where they were meeting their friends now."

Luka paused and looked down at her mittened hands. "Early yesterday morning I went to the other side of the Island and found the abandoned house they go to now in the same shape as the old one, bottles, old furniture, and other evidence of people staying there recently. I knew it was our brothers and their friends who had been there. It is very obvious they are bringing alcohol and prostitutes to the Island. Rose, my heart breaks for these poor girls who are not much older than us and living as prostitutes. They will do anything for a meal and liquor. How can they live such lives? How can our brothers promote such things?"

She began quietly crying again. Taking a shaky, deep breath, Luka continued. "I was walking back to the village when out of nowhere someone tackled me from behind and threatened me, telling me to never come to the house again, to stay where I belonged or I would be killed. His face was covered and I didn't know who it was. He held a knife to my throat and then cut my face with it as a warning." Again Luka covered her face and cried fresh tears.

Rose turned white as a sheet while Luka was talking. She put her arms tighter around her friend. "What did your mother and father say, Luka? How did you explain your face?"

"I stayed busy yesterday and wore a scarf around my parents when I was near them. I told them I was not feeling well and went to bed early, then rose before daylight and quickly did the chores and left before my parents were up." Luka sighed deeply and looked again in Rose's eyes. "Rose, I am scared to death. Do not go to the old house near the village nor pursue your brother to their new hiding place like I did. I don't want you hurt. You must not tell anyone about this. Even though I am terrified, I *have* to get help from the authorities at Seal Harbor. You have to understand. It's for our entire village. I will tell mother and father that a branch scraped my face when I was running after a hare. Don't say or do anything, Rose. For now, okay?" Luka said between her trembling.

Gently touching Luka's hurt face, Rose heard her friend's pleas to understand and not say anything. For now she would agree and later, when she could think clearly, she would figure out what to do. Luka had been through enough and Rose wouldn't add to Luka's worries. "I understand, Luka. I will stay quiet."

Remembering why she came to find Luka in the first place, Rose brightened. "Friend, I have some really good news. Maybe it will make you feel better. Uncle James came back from Seal Harbor last night and said his friend there told him that the missionaries were coming to Datka! They will be here tomorrow! God has heard our prayers, Luka, and is sending relief to us!"

Luka's face glowed with the much needed good news. "Oh, Rose, that is wonderful! Does the village know about this? It will really help lift the spirits of those who lost their homes!"

"You know how quickly news travels here. I came to tell you and found Ola, Lydia, and your mother discussing it when I arrived. They are all so excited. Luka, this is just what we need." She hugged her friend again. "Let's get you home and doctor your face."

The two girls walked arm in arm towards Luka's home unaware of the set of evil, black eyes that had been watching them from a safe distance away.

# CHAPTER 24

Eyes, blue as his cotton t-shirt, shone with excitement. It was moments like these that Gabriel Parker knew what he was made for. The small bush plane was descending, ready for landing on the Bering Sea near Datka Island in the Aleutian Island chain.

Gabe had prepared both day and night for the last few days for this moment. As one of the leaders of the relief team, he felt prepared for the weeks and months ahead. They would be full of work, purpose, and seeing his Aleutian family. It had been too long since Gabe had seen them. In three short years, he knew so much would have changed, mainly because the last time he was here he had just graduated from high school, just 18.

Now at 21, he had his associate's degree under his belt and was able to use it to bring much needed relief to these special people, not just work alongside his father as on prior trips, but to actually lead a team of people who would be looking to him for guidance and direction. As exciting as this was to Gabe, it was also a bit intimidating. But Gabe believed God had called him to this work, so he knew God would equip him as well.

Readying his body for the touch-down on the water's sparkling surface, Gabe peered out the small window at the shoreline of Datka Island. He could see men, women, and children all running towards the shore, ready to greet them. Excitement grew with each passing second; he couldn't get off the plane fast enough.

Gabe looked over at his friend and co-worker, Edward Hamilton, and saw that Ed was just as anxious as he was to be off the plane and on the ground with their friends. Gabe knew that not far behind in another bush plane, the Millers would soon be landing too. This would be a new adventure for them all, working closely with another family on the Island. The extra help would really be needed on this trip. Gabe was grateful for the Millers and their willingness to serve with them. After the last four days in Fairbanks at the AMRA headquarters, Gabe was ready to see the fruits of their hours of planning begin to take shape.

As soon as the small plane touched down and floated to shore, Gabe was the first to emerge from the plane. He stepped on the rocky shoreline and looked around him at the beautiful Alaskan landscape. Though a little foggy, the sun happened to be shining through the sparse fog today. The temperatures were mild for the Aleutians and the winds were calm. It was like God had special ordered the weather for them on the day of their flight.

Looking around him at the faces approaching the plane, Gabe saw some of the older familiar faces that had become so very dear to him. Aggie and James, sweet, old Ola and her daughter, Lydia and husband, Michael. Gabe noticed the little one in Michael's arms and assumed it was the toddler from his previous trips that Gabe had fallen in love with, little Lillian. She loved to follow Gabe around last time he was here, holding his hand. He knew she probably didn't even remember him. He saw Natalia, and holding tightly to her arm was Ivan walking slowly beside her. Gabe remembered Ivan had been very sick on their last trip; at least he was up and walking. He looked at the beautiful smiling faces of all ages and knew he would remember this moment forever.

Scanning the small crowd and seeing all of the precious ones before him, Gabe turned toward the sound of the other approaching bush plane. He knew that the Millers would be getting off any second and turned to help them. As he headed back towards the water, Gabe's eye caught a sight that made him gasp aloud. Tall and slim, the black-haired girl with breath-taking hazel green eyes set in a chiseled, lightly tanned face was moving towards them with a beautiful furry Malamute at her heels. Not only did her beauty and grace stop him in his tracks, but so did the feeling of familiarity, that he knew who she was, but couldn't quite place her.

Their eyes met at the same instant. Gabe could see that she too had been stopped in her tracks when she saw him, her mouth opening slightly in surprise, a slight frown crossed her pretty brow, then a tentative smile. He brought his attention back to the plane and the Millers. Gabe would have to find out later who she was, but for now unloading was the most important thing at hand.

The Millers disembarked from their small craft and looked around with admiring eyes at the gorgeous scenery surrounding them. Jade's green eyes sparkled with excitement as she approached the Aleutians, cautiously, yet confidently. She stood next to the Parkers and Ed waiting to be introduced to the group.

Rand quickly got the greetings underway. He and Becca hugged the few closest to them, then he backed up a few steps and said loudly to the smiling faces before him, "Hello, dear Aleutian family! We are so pleased to see you! What a surprise to see you all on the shore when we arrived! We have missed you so much. Becca, Gabe, and I have brought some new friends with us for this trip who will be working right alongside us. Please meet the Parkers, John, his wife, Jill, and daughter, Jade. They are from the Fairbanks mission team." Cheers and hellos rippled through the group as the Aleutians began greeting them all. As the excitement died down, the unloading process and placing the mission team in homes began. This would take some time to get them all settled.

In the fringes of the crowd, Gabe kept getting glimpses of the girl he had seen on the shore as she worked to locate the newly arrived families in homes. Like looking in an old photo album, a young girl's face appeared in his mind. Rose.....the sweet girl, just turned teen, quiet, shy, tall, always wanting to help out in any situation. Rose, that was her! Only she was much taller, even more strikingly beautiful and graceful. How old would she be now? Fifteen, sixteen? Gabe had to find her as soon as he was free.

Meanwhile, Ed was assigned to stay with Yuri and Michael's displaced family. The Parkers would be with Aggie and James. An elderly family, William and Grace, who lived in a larger home and who's children were grown and living on their own, took the Millers in. Food brought from the mission headquarters was distributed to these homes that would house the new-comers along with their luggage. Ed organized some of the teens to help him set up a place to unload and leave the construction tools and equipment until they were ready to use it. Evening was approaching and tomorrow would allow more time for organizing and meeting with the families of the village to assess the needs. Dinner had to be cooked and served and beds readied for the mission team. They were all both excited and exhausted from the days spent in preparation for this time on Datka.

After all had eaten dinner and were beginning to settle in for the evening, Gabe heard someone approaching William and Grace's yard. He looked up to see the girl from the shore with her dog. Instantly his suspicions were confirmed. It was Rose. She had a basket hanging from one arm as she tentatively approached Gabe. Neither could take their eyes off the other.

Rose was stunned at the handsome man before her. She remembered him quite well. He still looked much the same, only a little older. Gabriel. As a young girl and emerging teen she did her best to not be so obvious in trying to be wherever Gabe was. Realizing she was simply staring, Rose stammered, "I-I wanted to bring some extra bread that my mother made. She wanted to make sure there was enough food for everyone. If you need anything, please let us know and we will get it for you, or at least we will if we have it…." Rose cut her sentence off, knowing she was sounding foolish to her own ears. She quickly set the basket down and turned to leave.

"Wait! Rose, right? I remember you, only you have grown up in the last three years. You are Natalia and Ivan's daughter." Gabe smiled broadly at her.

Blushing, Rose said, "Yes, I'm Rose. And you are Gabriel. It has been a while since you were here. I, um, Datka Island is so very pleased that you and your team have come to our aid."

"Well, thank you, Rose, for the bread. We must get reacquainted in the days ahead." Gabe found himself staring again. She was beautiful and oh, so graceful. "Uh, well, I guess I need to rest up for tomorrow's work. See you in the morning."

"Yes, me too. Good night, Gabriel." Without looking back, Rose quickly turned away from him. Calling Stormy to her side, he watched her hurry back the way she had come.

Intrigue and fascination filled Gabe as he watched Rose walk away from him. He looked forward to the coming days with a new anticipation before him.

# CHAPTER 25

Thinking he was hearing angels singing, Ivan stirred from under the heavy fur blankets. He had a rough night two nights before, after the walk to the shore to greet the missionaries. Last night was easier for him, his coughing not as severe. He lay still for a while longer listening, his mind making the connection that it was his sweet Rose singing and not angels. She was up before all of them today, as she was most days. The sound of her softly singing was the only unusual thing about this morning. Rose usually awakened quietly so she didn't disturb the others still sleeping. Ivan pulled the blankets aside and slowly moved his tired body to a standing position. His Natalia had worked hard the last couple of weeks, and she was exhausted. She never complained, but he knew it. The quiet sounds of her soft snoring let him know she was still sound asleep.

Ivan eased himself to the kitchen doorway and stood watching his daughter. Her back was to him as she prepared the morning coffee. She hummed a beautiful ancient song taught to her by his own mother when Rose was a little girl. Ivan's thoughts of young Rose took him to long gone days, troubling days as he listened to the old song she hummed.

His deepest regret surfaced again. If he could go back to those days, he would do things so very differently.....

Ivan stepped off his fishing boat ready to see his sweet Natalia and son. Andrew made him proud, always wanting to please, willing to look after his mother when Ivan was gone on the overnight fishing trips. This time he had to be gone for several nights to sell his fish and furs on the mainland. He hated being gone overnight, but he had to provide for his little family. Tonight he would sleep peacefully in Natalia's arms. Only a little longer and he would be home. Ivan rounded a bend in the path and saw their humble house. He immediately knew something was wrong. No fire was lit; neither Natalia nor Andrew was in the yard doing chores or playing together. All was quiet. Maybe one of them was sick. He rushed the last few steps towards the front door. Inside Ivan found little Andrew sitting at the table with a cup of water and a piece of dry bread, not their usual meal for lunch. Natalia made sure they ate well each meal, not bread and water.

He knelt beside his son and looked at his red eyes and tear-stained face. "Andrew, what is wrong? Where is your mother?"

Andrew wiped his nose on his sleeve and grabbed Ivan around the neck. He let go to answer. "Father, she is in bed sick. Mother has been there since yesterday. She won't eat or drink."

Ivan rushed to their room and found Natalia in bed. He brushed the hair back from her face. "Natalia, I am home. Are you sick?" Her brow wasn't fevered to his touch.

Natalia grabbed his warm hands in her cold ones. "Ivan, you are home!" She hugged his neck tightly.

"I am here. Are you feeling poorly? Where do you hurt?" Worry creased his brow. He didn't understand what was going on.

Tears sprang to Natalia's eyes. "I am just very tired. I needed to rest today." She roused herself, seeming to come to life at the sight of him.

Confused, Ivan helped her up. Natalia went to Andrew. "Son, are you hungry? Let me fix you some lunch." She busied herself with preparing food for them all.

Ivan turned to leave the house to finish unloading his gear. Natalia almost shouted at him, fear all over her face. "Ivan, where are you going? Don't leave!"

"Just to get my gear, then I will be right back, Natalia." He spoke slowly to her, so very confused at her reaction.

She stopped what she was doing and said hastily, "I will help you."

"Fine, Natalia. Come help me. Andrew, finish your meal. We will return soon."

As soon as they were outside and alone, Ivan turned to Natalia, grabbing her shoulders. "What is wrong, my sweet wife? What has happened? You are so afraid! This is not like you."

*Her response was almost harsh, something he was unaccustomed to, coming from her. "Nothing! Just don't leave us again, even if we must starve to death!" She rushed ahead of him towards his fishing gear and grabbed an armload leaving Ivan behind, dumbfounded, unsure of what had happened, but determined never to leave his precious ones alone again.*

Taking a deep breath to erase the memory, he couldn't remove it all from his mind. Ivan remembered it didn't take long to hear from his friends about the French botanist and his boatman that came to Datka. He heard that Natalia cooked their meals for them during their stay for money. When he asked her about this, Natalia gave him a quick account of it and retrieved the money she had made from a jar on a shelf. She rushed from the room after almost tossing the money to him as if it were on fire.

Ivan wondered for weeks what happened while he was away. At times, his mind would play tricks on him, making him have thoughts of her being unfaithful, or to the other extreme, her being abused in some way by one of the men. Natalia refused to talk to him about those few days, cutting his questions off or changing the subject.

A couple of months later, Natalia told him she was expecting a baby. When she gave him the news of Andrew's expected arrival, she was elated and giddy, talking every day about the baby and planning for its birth. This time was different; she wasn't happy. She seemed almost regretful of the new baby growing inside of her, something he never thought possible of Natalia. Her pregnancy sent her to bed most days, sick and tearful. Nights he would hear her pacing the floor, sobbing quietly. The few times he tried to comfort Natalia, she would turn away. Eventually he withdrew from his wife, mostly out of frustration and confusion.

Several months later, Ivan's deepest, unspoken fears were confirmed. Rose looked nothing like them. The only resemblance was her dark hair. Rose's eye color wasn't the Aleutian dark brown, nor did she have their darker skin tone. She was a long, lean, light-skinned, baby with eyes the color of moss with brown and gold flecks.

Never did he speak to Natalia of his fear. If he spoke it aloud, surely it would be true. At her birth, Natalia changed. She took one look at her daughter and Natalia was her old self again. He was the one to change. At Rose's birth and as she grew older, Ivan knew deep in his heart that Rose was not his baby. He could never believe, even if he tried to convince himself, that Natalia had been unfaithful. What happened had been his fault; he hadn't been home to protect her. Now he lived with a constant reminder of his failure.

Now, Ivan's only regret was that at Rose's birth and during the first two years of her life his heart was hardened to the little girl who wasn't really his daughter. She hadn't done anything wrong; she just reminded him daily of how he had failed his family. But Ivan would always remember the day that his heart changed, the day the walls fell down and he accepted that though she wasn't of his flesh, she was still his Rose.

Rose had fallen and cut her tiny hand on a rock. Instead of running, crying to Natalia, she looked up with her soft green eyes at him and said through her tears, "Papa, me hurt. Kiss it." It was the first time she had addressed him, much less come to him for comfort. Natalia had always been her first and only choice, but that day he was amazed that one so small could destroy such high, thick walls as those around his heart with five short words.

Coming back to the present, Ivan stood quietly until a cough forced its way out of his body. Rose turned at the noise and came to his side. With a quick kiss on his weathered cheek, she said, "Father, I'm sorry. Did I wake you?"

"No, Rose. An angel's voice did, or what I thought was an angel. Instead I find something sweeter. It was you singing. What has my quiet one singing so early in the morning?" He smiled at his daughter and sat down at the table.

Handing her father his coffee, Rose blushed and said quickly, "Oh, I just awoke in a cheerful mood. Nothing special." She turned away, afraid her thoughts of Gabe would betray her and be written across her forehead. "How do you feel today, better than yesterday? You should have stayed home instead of making the walk to greet the missionaries. Are you ready for your breakfast? I hope the missionaries brought more medicine for your coughing. Is mother still sleeping?" Pausing to breathe, Rose stopped the flow of words, the tell-tale sign of her distraction and momentary discomfort.

Ivan grinned to himself, relishing the fact that he knew his daughter so very well. Something, or someone, had her cheerful enough to hum and sing this morning. "To answer your questions: good, yes, yes, and yes." Her father's eyes twinkled with humor. At Rose's look of confusion, he cleared his answer up. "I feel good today. Yes, better than yesterday. Yes, I am ready for breakfast, and yes, your mother is still sleeping." Ivan and Rose both laughed at once, a sound that was music to his ears. Growing more serious he simply said, "Rose, I love you."

"I love you, too, Father." Rose set his bowl of porridge before him and sat across from him with her coffee ready for a moment the two of them didn't have often enough. Rose spoke in hushed tones so she wouldn't awaken her tired mother. While Ivan ate, Rose filled him in on the last two days of the Island's activities and the plans being made by the missionaries.

# CHAPTER 26

Gabe rose early on the third day since their arrival on Datka Island. The first two days were spent unloading and organizing the tools and supplies for construction. The Parkers had also spent time introducing the Millers and reacquainting themselves with their Aleutian family and settling into their temporary locations.

Gabe knew there were many obstacles still to overcome. He was planning on a return trip to Fairbanks to bring back more building materials and supplies for the school and homes. Yes, logistics was his niche. He felt confident in his abilities to make this mission trip a success. That, and the wonderful team with him.

Two things did trouble Gabe however. The unspoken friction between Ed and Jade and the reactions of several of the young adults he had seen on the day they arrived. Right now, Jade and Ed needed to be at peace with each other especially since he had planned for them to work together on a few projects. Maybe he should talk to each of them privately. Ed seemed completely enamored with Jade and completely frustrated with her at the same time. One minute he was following her around like a puppy, and the next he was making a hasty exit if she got within ten feet of him.

Gabe couldn't blame Ed for his reactions to the beautiful, intriguing Jade. She was funny, pretty, smart, and a Christian. But she also, in Gabe's opinion, was a bit too judgmental or almost snobby at times. Gabe quickly reprimanded himself for such thoughts about her. He was also uncomfortable with her seeming to want to be wherever he was. He thought to himself, *Gabe, you're being ridiculous. What guy wouldn't want her attention? Plus your mind's just playing tricks on you. Jade's just being friendly.* Either way, he didn't want to see his best buddy hurt by Jade.

But for now, he had other things that demanded his concentration. Gabe needed two people to work with some of the Aleutian school teachers to determine what repairs needed to be made and what school books, school supplies, and other damaged items needed to be replaced so he would know exactly what to bring back on his return trip. Now he was questioning assigning Jade and Ed to this task; but, then again, working together could be the best thing for those two.

Gabe's thoughts returned to the day of their arrival on the Island. He and Rand were talking to their Aleutian friends shortly after landing and something or someone caught his eye. Gabe noticed what looked like several young people watching the new-comers from about 100 feet away. The group obviously did not want to be noticed. They were trying to stay out of sight behind some low trees. Without looking too apparent, Gabe slipped his sunglasses back on and angled himself to get a better look while still conversing with the others. Rand picked up on what Gabe had seen and glanced in the same direction. Later that afternoon, after comparing notes, Rand and Gabe had seen the same thing, probably four or five young people, males and females maybe in their twenty's watching from afar. They wondered why the young people didn't come greet them with the rest of the Aleutians. Not long after Gabe and Rand spotted them, they all ducked back through the trees. Gabe was curious who they were and planned on asking around later.

But for now, his focus needed to be elsewhere. Gabe saw his parents and Ed headed towards their designated meeting place. The elderly couple, William and Grace, who had taken the Millers in, offered their kitchen area as a place for the mission team to hold their daily meetings before work began. Grace was enjoying cooking for them and bustling around doing her best to make them comfortable. Her coffee was hot and her bread always warm, both a blessed start to their day. When they all had found their spots around the table, Gabe began assigning the work for the day.

He had turned the burned fishing boats shed and home repairs over to John and Randall, so John quickly laid out the day's plan. They were to assess needs and damages, create lists of what Gabe needed to bring back to the Island, and organize a work crew to remove the ruined and fire damaged sections of the houses, all in preparation for the rebuilding process.

Jill and Becca were in charge of going to each family whose house was burned down and of making lists of all household needs. While at each house, the women would also determine if there were any sick ones in the home and list what medicines and first aid supplies were lacking for their care.

Lastly, Gabe assigned Jade and Ed to work with Helena and Iris, both Aleutian school teachers. This team would create lists of the damaged school's needs. Gabe glanced at Jade and Ed both and saw a mixture of elation, disappointment, frustration, and resignation cross their faces. *These two will just have to learn to work together and make the best of it,* Gabe reasoned.

Ed looked over at Jade and drawled, "Well, little lady, I guess we've got our work cut out for us." Glad for the opportunity to work with Jade and hopefully get to know her a little better, Ed determined to make the best of things. Maybe they just got off on the wrong foot and today he could do something about that.

Jade sighed and looked at Ed, "I guess so, Tex. Let me grab my gear." Jade went and spoke to her parents for a few minutes then headed back inside to get her backpack. Coming back outdoors, she didn't see Ed anywhere. Going in search of him, Jade rounded the corner of the house and heard Gabe's voice and a female voice. She paused out of sight and listened in on the conversation.

Gabe was saying, "I thought you and I could float around and help out wherever extra hands are needed today with all the projects. I feel sure you will see some things that I have overlooked since you actually live here and I don't. Plus, we can get reacquainted while we work. That is, if you don't already have your day planned."

Straining to hear the response, Jade heard the girl's soft answer. "My day is free. That sounds great, Gabriel. Let me tell my mother where I will be and then we can meet up at my house after you finish here."

Gabe spoke to the girl. "Great! I look forward to working with you today, Rose."

Jade walked around the corner in time to see the young woman's blushing face. Rose didn't answer Gabe, but instead turned and walked away.

Gabe turned and frowned at Jade and the interruption. Jade knew better than to say a word to him; her emotions would spill out for sure. She felt the bitter jealousy creep up her chest, into her throat, and lodge in her mind. She walked away chiding herself. *Why should I be jealous of her? Of an Indian girl? Gabe is just being nice to her and nothing more. There's nothing in common between them like there is with Gabe and I. So settle down, Jade.* She lifted up her chin and determined to get through the rest of the day and not concern herself with silly girls and Gabe. He would see soon enough that they were made for each other. At least to be great friends, and who knew where that could lead?

# CHAPTER 27

Still not seeing Ed around, Jade headed in the direction of the school. There she met up with Helena, Iris, and Ed in the schoolyard. They spent the day going over the needs with the two teachers. Jade's heart was filled with compassion for the teachers and students and their ability to run a school with such meager supplies. Not even a chalkboard or enough books for each student to have their own or enough paper and pencils to go around! She was determined to see that the school would be well-stocked with more than just the basic necessities. Surprisingly Jade enjoyed the work there. She connected with the teachers and even found herself laughing at Ed's silly jokes. It was obvious he was very intelligent, though he didn't flaunt it. Ed asked many questions she would have never thought of that gave them even more insight to the students' and teachers' needs.

The morning sped by. The little group decided to break for lunch, so the two teachers headed to their homes. Jade and Ed had brought their own lunches with them.

Ed picked up his bag and asked Jade, "How does a walk to the shore for a picnic sound? I could use the exercise and fresh air away from the burnt smell. It's not too windy so this might be a good chance to go."

Jade hesitated, catching herself from wishing Gabe had offered her the invitation. "Sure. The sun will feel good. I'm game if you are."

The two walked quietly to the shore taking in the sights and sounds of Datka Island, the sedge-lined, rocky path, the sounds of ptarmigan mothers calling to their chicks, little rabbits scurrying to get out of their way, and the feel of the warm sun on their shoulders taking the chill from the slight breeze. Ed loved everything about this day, helping those he cared about, working with Jade, the beauty of the Island. They engaged in small talk for a bit and ate their lunch sitting on a huge boulder by the shore.

Ed decided it was time to not be so tense and just be himself. He thought of a million questions for Jade when he lay in bed at night. For the life of him he couldn't remember those questions, so he asked her the first thing he thought of. "So tell me Jade, how do you see your future turning out? Family, career, missions work like your parents?"

She slowly blushed and subconsciously reached for her jade green cross around her neck before answering. Her thoughts had once again drifted towards a special guy with brilliant blue eyes. "Oh, I don't know." Jade squirmed uncomfortably under Ed's gaze. To divert his attention from her, Jade asked, "What about you, Tex?"

Ed loved the nickname Jade had given him. His heart beat a little faster each time she called him that. Silently he mused, *Well, I didn't know I could make Jade blush. Maybe she is warming up to me.* He looked into her beautiful green eyes and spoke softly and slowly. "I see myself with a lovely, Godly girl, one who wants to find out with me what adventure God would have for the two us. A girl who can be my best friend, who loves nature, helping people, laughing, traveling…maybe someone a lot like you, Jade." He flashed his half-grin, embarrassed but satisfied that he had been bold enough to be honest.

Ed expected Jade's blush to deepen on her pretty face, but instead her face paled within seconds as his words sank in. Seeing her demeanor completely change, Ed became alarmed at his outspokenness. "Oh, Jade. I'm sorry; I overstepped my bounds. I-I- didn't mean to make you uncomfortable. I wasn't talking about me and *you*….just someone *like* you. Look, Jade, we got off on the wrong foot when we first met and I just thought…."

Finally she blurted, "Ed, stop! Yes, we're friends, but don't you see, it wouldn't work. We could never be more than friends, and you could never be more than friends with someone *like* me."

Confused, Ed became quiet for a minute. Finding his courage again, he asked, "But why, Jade? I don't get it."

She jumped up from the rock and wheeled around to face Ed head on. Looking at him like a child who just couldn't get her explanation, she sighed and rolled her eyes in frustration at his confusion. With visions of another man flitting through her mind, Jade spoke a bit too harshly than she even intended. "Ed, we aren't the same! We aren't like-minded! I want someone like me, a guy who's lived his whole life serving God, who has remained pure in every area, was raised in a Christian home, and-and someone on the same level as me! Ugh! Ed, why do you make this so hard?" During her speech, Jade began throwing her things into her bag, readying to leave.

Ed was astonished, even appalled, at the words that came from his beautiful Jade's mouth. *How dare she!* Ed thought to himself. *How could she say such things?*

Hitting him like a ton of bricks, Ed got the full message in her words. He wasn't "good enough" in Jade's eyes. She had just painted the picture of her perfect man, someone actually like Gabe. Why hadn't he seen it before?

He got up and walked over to a nearby tree, just to get away from Jade for a second before he spoke. He could hear her gathering her lunch things and her bag.

Jade could see the impact her words had on Ed and didn't want to hurt him, just make him see what she meant. She softened a bit. "Look, Ed. I like you. I don't mean to hurt you, but you have to see we aren't the same." She spoke quietly, gently, but her words still felt like daggers to his freshly wounded heart.

Slowly, Ed turned to face Jade again. Looking into her eyes, Ed said quietly, "You know, you're right. We aren't the same." His shoulders slumped in sadness and he breathed a very deep sigh.

Jade smiled and felt better for the moment. He was getting it after all. "Oh Ed, I'm glad you understand." Jade took a couple of steps towards him and reached a hand out to touch him on the arm, but Ed quickly held up a hand to stop her.

"Jade, I have liked you a lot since the day I first saw you walk across the runway to meet our plane. But I have to tell you, little lady, *you* don't get it. You are right. We *are* different, but not like you think. You see, I've learned something lately. Even though I may have a very ugly, dirty, messed up past and made *many* wrong choices, I am no more a sinner than you are. I wasn't raised in a Christian home, I didn't go to church until three years ago, but that doesn't make me *less* of a Christian than you, Jade. Don't *you* see? It's not about upbringing or past actions or how *holy* a person lives. It's the heart of a person, Jade. And right now, your heart looks a lot like my past life!"

Her jaw dropped open at his words. Jade put her hands on her hips and opened her mouth to retaliate, but Ed wasn't done. "Your pride and self-righteousness are as bad as all my years of drunkenness and wrong choices. Now, I'm sorry to end our conversation this way, but I need to leave. I'll see you later." With that he stalked off, leaving Jade utterly speechless.

Tears quickly sprung to Jade's eyes and she dashed them away along with the sting of the truth of his words. Unable to head back to the village at the moment, Jade walked down the shore a little way, her mind spinning with emotions. *How dare he! No one has ever spoken to me like that! I didn't deserve that treatment. I was only honestly answering his question and look what I get in return! Ed doesn't understand; we aren't the same! I need someone like me, like Gabe, to spend my life with, not a cowboy with a past as dirty as the bottom of his boots! Gabe would never have spoken to me that way. And now I've lost Ed as a friend. But a real friend would never be so mean, so brutal! Pride? Self-righteousness? I was just being factual and honest, real with him!* Jade's pace quickened with the racing of her thoughts. *Ed can't even begin to compare the two of us. I've lived a good life and deserve someone who has done the same for me, for his future. Even if I were prideful or self-righteous, it's* nothing *compared to Ed's past! It's not the same!*

Jade stopped at the water's edge and made her mind stop as well. This was getting her nowhere. She bent down to tie her shoe and then head back, not feeling an ounce better than she had before. She was also trying to drown out the words floating through her mind. Words from a couple of Bible verses she knew.

*....For all have sinned and come short of the glory of God....*

*....Our righteousness is but filthy rags....*

*********************

Leaning back on his heels, Ed threw a small stick into their evening fire. He loved this part of the day, relaxing his tired body by the fire, laughing with his American and Aleutian friends, enjoying the cold, crisp Alaskan air. Tonight was different though. He couldn't settle down like usual. Ed's thoughts and emotions were too weighty.

Rand knew Ed well enough to know something was wrong. He, Ed, and a few of the Aleutian men had worked all day removing the burned down sections of the school. It would take them several more days to prepare it for construction. Ed had been unusually quiet all day. Rand couldn't bring Ed out of his stupor no matter how hard he tried.

Gabe was sitting away from the group telling stories to Rose, Luka, and some of the younger children. The Miller family and Becca had just turned in for the night so Rand saw an opportunity for he and Ed to talk.

Believing there was no better way than to just address something head-on, Rand chose to do so with Ed. "So tell me, Ed. What's been eating at you all day? You've been really quiet."

Ed sighed deeply. "Oh, I don't know. Just tired I guess."

Rand knew better. "Look, Son. I've known you long enough to be able to tell the difference between 'Tired Ed' and 'Troubled Ed.' So spill it." Rand nudged Ed's boot with his own.

Ed looked up at Rand's sincere face. "Okay, I'll spill. It's not pretty though." He paused to gather his thoughts. "Yesterday, you know Jade and I worked together at the school. We stopped for lunch and walked down to the shore to eat. As usual, I don't know when to keep my mouth shut so I asked her a question which I thought was harmless. Apparently she didn't and it ruffled her feathers. She said some things...I said some things...she's upset with me....I'm mad at her. End of story."

Rand broke a stick into tiny pieces while he listened to Ed. "How do you feel about Jade, Ed?"

The tall Texan quickly stood up and looked at Rand, asking a bit roughly, "What's *that* got to do with anything?" A deep furrow marked his tanned brow.

Rand stifled a grin. "It may have everything to do with this situation. I don't mean to pry, but I need to know how you feel if you want my advice. If not, I understand it's none of my business."

Ed simmered down quickly. "Sorry, Randall; I must be more mad that I realize." Taking a deep breath, Ed spoke his heart. "If I trust anyone, it's you, Rand. So here it is. Since the first day I laid eyes on the little lady, Jade has driven me crazy. One second I want to be by her side and the next, I want to run from her screaming. She's beautiful, funny, smart, godly, frustrating, annoying, and down right........ wonderful! Do you see my problem? *I* don't even know how I feel about her! All I know is I want to be a friend to her and I think she wants to be a friend to me, but who knows?" Ed paused for a breath. "Yesterday I asked her how she saw her future playing out and next thing you know I was mad and saying things to her I shouldn't have. She spouted off at me too and I left her on the shore fuming."

"Tell me what she said and maybe I can help shed some light on this." Rand looked sympathetically at Ed.

Ed relayed their conversation on the shore word for word. It had replayed itself over and over so many times in his head, he knew their conversation by heart.

Rand looked up at Ed's pleading eyes, eyes that spoke of his need for Rand to help him see the truth. "Son, it sounds like you have a really strong interest in Jade. Maybe even as more than a friend. You obviously brought up a topic that she's adamant about, her future and her mate. I don't agree with her on everything she said and that's not my place to tell her so. In my opinion, you spoke the truth to her and it wasn't well received. People don't always like the truth, much less the one who delivers it, if it's something they don't *want* to hear. Give her time and space to cool off. Pray for her. Be kind to her when you two are together. And focus on *why* you are here at Datka....to serve."

Ed looked down at his scuffed boots. "But why do I have to pray for her and be kind? Why can't I just stay away from her? Truthfully, I don't *want* to be kind to her. She wasn't exactly kind to me. The girl hates me!"

"It's your choice, Ed. But it's what the Bible says to do. 'Bless you enemies. Pray for those who persecute you.' You might be surprised how it turns out." With a sound pat on Ed's back, Randall left him to his thoughts.

Expecting to receive a gentle rebuke for his response to Jade, Ed got the opposite. Randall agreed with what he had said. Ed also didn't expect to be told to be nice to her, to bless her, to pray for her, all the things he *didn't* want to do right now. Instead he wanted to keep away from Jade and any future arguments they may have. How do you be nice to someone who has made you feel like a pile of cow manure? Ed knew she had hurt his pride and his feelings. He also knew his pity-party today had done nothing to improve his state of mind. Doing what now came naturally to him, Ed prayed.

*Ok, God, I know Rand's got a point. That is what the Bible says, but how on earth can I do such a thing? This is where I need Your help. So first I will ask for the grace and ability to be kind to Jade. Next I ask that You bless her. Help her see You and Your truth in this. I know for some reason our paths have crossed and I believe it's for more than rubbing each other the wrong way. Help me be a friend to Jade. And help me sort out my mixed up emotions. In Your Son's name, amen.*

Ed felt at peace again. Talking with Rand and talking with God always helped. And tomorrow was a new day. He looked up into the late night sky and felt God was with him. As Ed stood to go to bed, he was grateful that he lingered these last ten minutes to pray. He was dazzled at the sight before his eyes, the brilliant blues, greens, reds, and purples of the dancing Northern Lights. Yes, God was with him even here on a remote island in Alaska.

# CHAPTER 28

Fuming at herself a day later, Jade decided the best course of action was to get her mind off her and Ed's fight and on to something that would distract her. After all she was here to work, not argue with a handsome guy. Jade fiddled with her green cross necklace, a constant reminder of who she had devoted her life to years ago and also of what she wanted in her future. *Why is it so hard to believe I can have someone who has done the same as I have in committing to love and serve Christ? I won't give up on that ideal,* Jade mused.

Sighing loudly, she went in search of the little children to play with. She had some free time on her hands and nothing assigned to do for the afternoon so Jade decided to do one of her favorite things, spend time with the little ones. From the AMRA headquarters, the team had brought a basketball, a soccer ball, jacks, little dolls, yo-yos, and other small inexpensive toys for the children. The team felt like Santa Clause as they would surprise the children with some new trinket every few days to enjoy. Jade decided she would bring out something new to give them.

Heading to their stash of toys packed away, Jade heard children's shouts and laughter. She came upon a scene that made her both smile and frown within seconds of each other.

The children had obviously been introduced to basketball; there was a make-shift woven basket hanging from a tree with the bottom cut out and a dozen boys and girls taking turns shooting the ball. They loudly cheered each other's attempts to make a basket and laughed and clapped with excitement, their faces lit up with sheer joy.

Gabe caught the ball and began speaking to Rose. She was almost as tall as Gabe and for the first time Jade took notice of how strikingly beautiful and graceful she was. Gabe had the ball and was attempting to talk Rose into trying to make a basket. She ducked her head, but finally gave in. Gabe stood behind Rose and reached around her to position her hands with the ball in correct form. He showed her how to push off from a slight crouch and shoot towards the basket. After two attempts, Rose scored a basket. She giggled and clapped with delight, like a little girl, her face glowing with her achievement and the praise of the little ones dancing around her.

The old familiar jealousy crept up inside of Jade again. All it took was watching Gabe's admiration and attention he showed Rose. Laughing with Rose, Gabe patted her on the back. He looked around and noticed Jade standing off from the group.

"Hi, Jade! Want to join us?" Gabe took a few steps in her direction and tossed the basketball to Jade.

She deftly caught it and replied, "Sure, why not? It might help me warm up a bit from this chilly temperature today." Being very athletic, Jade was great at almost any sport she played, so basketball was a breeze for her. She successfully made five back to back shots sending the children into another round of clapping and cheering.

Gabe shot her a look, "Impressive!" He immediately noticed her slight blush at his comment.

Jade was now swarmed by the children, all asking her to show them how to shoot like she did. She enjoyed the attention from them and giving them a few pointers. Gabe stood back and let her have some time with the children, watching Jade's patience and how she made sure to include each child. Gabe thought, *She is good with them. Jade will definitely be an asset to VBS in the months to come. Rose will be quite a bit of help too in this area.*

Turning to speak to Rose about his VBS ideas, he found that she was gone. Frowning, Gabe looked around and couldn't understand why she would leave when she was having such a good time.

With the game still underway, Jade could feel Gabe's admiring eyes on her as she made the goals and played with the children. She loved the feeling of his admiration. Jade looked up to see a frown on his face and that he was distracted for a moment. He bent to ask one of the little boys, "Did you see Rose leave? Where did she go?"

Smiling widely at his hero, the little boy looked up at Gabe. "I saw her run down that path, Mr. Gabe, but I don't know where she went."

Gabe ruffled the boy's hair. "Thanks, buddy." He stayed for a while longer and played basketball with the group, but at this point, he missed almost every shot of the ball he tried to make.

*********************

Rose hurried down the path after she had stolen silently away from the basketball game. Her face was aflame at her behavior and thoughts. *How could I let myself have feelings for someone like Gabe? Even worse, why would I think he would be interested in me when the beautiful Jade is around? I am such a foolish, silly girl. I must keep my distance before my heart tells me to do otherwise. Gabe is only being nice to me like he is the other little children.*

Headed home to remind herself who she was and where she belonged, Rose entered the house and was instantly alarmed. She heard her father's deep, raspy cough from the front doorway. She ran to her parents' bedroom and instantly froze. Her mother was crying softly and placing a cool cloth on Ivan's forehead.

Her shoulders shaking gently, Natalia was talking to her husband in hushed tones. "Ivan, please try to drink this medicine. Becca gave me a bottle yesterday for you to try. She unpacked it and brought it right over when I told her about the last two rough nights you had. It will help you if you drink it. Please."

Ivan's watery eyes looked into his beautiful Natalia's. "My sweet wife, it is too late. But for you I will drink it. Just let me catch my breath."

Panic rose within Natalia. "Don't say that, Ivan. It isn't too late! You will be fine now that we have good medicine." She lifted Ivan's frail shoulders and spooned the medicine into his mouth.

Rose stepped to the bedside. Making herself ask the dreaded question, she said softly, "Mother, is he worse now? Father had shown signs of improvement only weeks ago."

Natalia hung her head, unable to look into Rose's eyes. "I know, Rose, but the last two days have been very, very difficult for him."

Hot tears filled Rose's eyes. "What can I do? I have been too busy to notice!" Flinging herself on her dear father's chest, Rose sobbed, "Oh, Father, I am so sorry. I didn't know you were this bad."

"Dear Rose. It happened suddenly. I will be fine. Do not worry." He reached up a weathered hand and touched her hair. A series of racking coughs shook Ivan's body as both mother and daughter struggled to help him through them. Finally Ivan lay back down on the bed. Beads of sweat covered his forehead. His old, wrinkled hands trembled at the pain in his chest. He whispered, "Please, I just need to sleep awhile." Ivan closed his eyes for several minutes.

Suddenly he opened them and grasped Natalia and Rose's hands. "My sweet girls." Tears came to Ivan's dark brown eyes. They could barely hear his words. "I love you both so much. You need to know I don't have long."

At their protests, Ivan said, "No. Let me speak. I have to leave you soon. Tell Andrew I want to speak to him very soon. I will be ready to leave this old body but sad to be away from you both for a while. We will be together again one day. That is our hope in Christ." He then closed his eyes and settled into a fitful sleep. Natalia laid her head on his chest and wept quietly.

Watching her parents a moment longer, Rose felt like her chest would explode if she stayed in the house another second. Her father was dying? Yes, he had been sick and had some very bad days but this....maybe she had denied it all along. But the missionaries had brought medicine for him. He *had* to recover!

Rose stumbled out of her house with tears coursing down her cheeks. She didn't see Gabe standing a few feet away. He had come in search of Rose after she left the basketball game.

Noticing her distress, Gabe quickly approached Rose. "What happened? Are you okay? Rose, tell me." She only covered her face and cried as she stood before him.

Embarrassed at her tears, sorrow for her father, her need to be *away* from Gabe and not any closer to him, all made her take flight. Feeling like a helpless child and completely confused by her tumultuous emotions, Rose did what her body told her to, she ran. Rose let out a heart-wrenching sob and took off blindly through the trees. Her aching heart felt like it would burst at any second. She didn't need Gabe's pity, his questions. She just needed to escape the pain she was feeling. With the low sedges scraping against her clothes, Rose couldn't stop running.

Gabe was right behind her. "Rose, stop! Please! What is wrong? Rose!" She was more familiar with the terrain than he was and was much more sure-footed on the rocky ground. Gabe would lose her for a few seconds then be right behind her again. Rose was fast! She rounded a corner and he lost sight of her again.

Then like a slow-motion movie, it happened. First, Gabe heard the sharp crack, like a tree limb breaking. He hesitated for a second until the louder crack and shrill scream reached his ears. Adrenaline pushed Gabe forward on winged feet. The piercing, fearful scream tore at his heart. *Rose is hurt!! Oh, dear God, not sweet Rose!* Gabe couldn't see where it came from.

The next frame in this slow-motion movie that Gabe seemed to be trapped in revealed a picture before his eyes of long fingers, reaching for something, anything to grasp. Then in a split second Gabe remembered the dream! The scream, the loud cracking noise, a hand reaching for his....he now knew Rose was the one in his dream. He could see clearly what had happened; Rose had stepped upon ice too thin to hold her. The crack was just like in his dream, ear-splitting, loud, and the screams as heart-wrenching and surreal. Only now it was real! It was sweet Rose in the icy water, grasping at the slippery edge for something to hold onto, frantic, struggling, gasping, and calling for help.

Gabe immediately said a quick prayer, "God help me help Rose!" He saw a long, large branch nearby and grabbed it in his hands. Laying flat on his belly, Gabe yelled at Rose as he pushed the branch to the water's edge. "Rose, listen to me! I need you to grab the branch and I will pull you out. Calm down and reach for the branch in front of you. I will help you, Rose!"

Rose frantically grabbed at the branch and on her third attempt she had a tight hold on it. Gabe slowly inched closer for a better grip. He talked to her calmly the entire time as he struggled to pull her panicked body out. Gabe was equally afraid he would fall through the ice too, and they would both die. Silently he prayed, *God, please, no! Don't let my life or Rose's end this way. Save us, please. Be our Rescuer! We need You.*

Slowly, carefully, he pulled her to him by the branch. Then wrapping both arms around a now silent, shaking Rose, he dragged both of them away from the ice. Removing his coat and wrapping it around her, Gabe lifted Rose into his arms and ran as fast as he could back to the village.

# CHAPTER 29

After a day's separation from Jade, Ed had cooled down a bit. He had been praying for her as Rand had suggested and was beginning to see that it was very difficult to be mad or upset with someone when your focus was on praying for them. The two had been assigned to work together today with the rest of the group to begin the clean-up of the burned homes. New construction was at a standstill until this stage was completed. All hands were needed for this project. The sun had decided to make another welcome appearance, and the day had warmed up to 57 degrees. The temperature was perfect for a day of hard, physical labor.

Ed approached the gathering group and said his hellos. He greeted the men with handshakes then turned to the ladies.

With a quick peck on Becca's cheek and a friendly glance in Jill's direction, he drawled, "Morning, Mrs. Bee. Howdy, Mrs. Jill."

With a glance at Jade, Ed said, "Morning, Jade." She gave him a cold smile in return. *This is going to be harder than I thought. She's as cold as an Alaskan icicle,* Ed thought to himself.

Gabe and John quickly laid out the day's clean-up plan, projecting it would take them and the other volunteers from the community about three to four days to remove and burn the remaining rubble. The days were flying by too quickly. After their first week in Fairbanks preparing for the trip to the Island, and the last two weeks almost over, Gabe felt the pressure to get the clean-up completed. In a few days, he wouldn't have Ed or his parents' help until they returned after school let out the end of May. The Parkers would stay on the Island with Gabe, but all three would make a return trip for one week to Fairbanks for more supplies and tools. That would then give them about five weeks before Ed and his parents returned for the summer months.

Gathering lunches, drinks, tools, and various other items for the project, the crew headed first for the homes that needed tearing down. Ed knew the hard work would be good for his mind and heart today. Confusion had set in the last day or so, this unnatural obsession over what Jade thought about him, dealing with emotions over a girl that he had never experienced before, and *why* Jade mattered so very much to him.

Before giving his life to Christ, Ed hadn't given girls much thought, except how an evening out with one could benefit him that night. After meeting the Parkers and learning from Rand and Becca's example of what a relationship should be like, Ed came to believe that girls were something that he didn't need to worry about. He began to see them as God's creation, special, unique, individuals with *hearts* and not just *bodies*. Ed had chosen to trust God with this area of his life, knowing God had that perfect girl out there for him and would cause their paths to cross at the right time.

So why the obsession with Jade? Ed knew she *definitely* wasn't the one for him. They couldn't even share the same air without getting crossways with each other.

While mulling all of this over in his mind, Ed had been tearing down and raking up burned debris from the house they were working on. He and John had started clearing out the space on this particular house while others were assigned to do the same for the other closely laid out houses. They had two people working on each one and were hoping with the beautiful, sunny, calm weather that today they would finish this part of the project and have the rubble burned by sundown.

John glanced in Ed's direction. "Ed, you are very quiet this morning. You've been tearing down and tossing the rubble so fast my eyes can't keep up with your movements. You okay? You're working like a man trying to take out his frustrations. And that frown on your face is going to be permanent if you don't relax a bit. Why so tense?" John propped his arm on his shovel and eyed Ed.

Ed looked up from his work and knew John was right. Better to take out his frustrations on a heap of rubble than a person. He took a deep breath and leaned on his rake. He shot a quick telling glance in Jade's direction that John didn't miss. "I don't know John. Maybe I'm not resting well. Need some water? I think I will get me some."

"Sure, Ed. That sounds good." John sat down on a nearby stump and watched the young man walk over to the water cooler. He saw Ed glance Jade's way again.

She was helping on another house not 100 yards away. John was proud of his daughter and her diligence and work ethic. Jade loved helping others and was willing to do whatever was needed. She paused from working and looked up, her face red from exertion. Her smile lit up her pretty face. She was talking to one of the Aleutians and reached a hand over and placed it on the woman's arm. God had blessed him and Jill with such a sweet-hearted girl. John glanced back at Ed. He had poured two cups of water and was headed for Jade, not John, with the second one. John smiled to himself as he watched the scene play out.

Ed remembered Rand's words. *Show her kindness.* Not what he wanted to do. Regardless, Ed decided to take Jade a cup of water. He watched her gentle ways with the woman she was talking to and her beautiful smile. Jade glanced up and saw Ed coming her way. Her smile fell and she unconsciously reached up for her jade green cross necklace.

Ed held out the cup of water to Jade. "You looked like you could use a drink, so I brought you some water." His hand was suspended in mid air and Jade just looked at the cup a moment.

"Thanks." Her eyes took on a cool glance, and no smile reached her lips. She took the cup from Ed. "I'm fine for now." Jade set it down on a large boulder, untouched.

"Ok. Well, then." Dejected, Ed slowly, almost imperceptibly, shook his head and walked away from Jade. His frown from earlier had returned. He quickly downed his cup of water and wadded the paper cup in his hand.

John's thoughts of pride in his daughter were now clouded with a touch of disappointment. *Why did she just treat Ed like that? That wasn't Jade's usual demeanor. She was always kind and respectful to others, not this haughty attitude.* John felt sorry for Ed for a brief moment.

Ed headed back to the water cooler and poured another cup. He walked straight for John. "Here you go, John." Ed stole one more glance in Jade's direction. She was no longer engaged in conversation with the Aleutian woman but sat off to herself fingering her cross. She tossed a look in Ed's direction and quickly turned her head when she saw the two men watching her.

John looked at Ed. "If I didn't know better, I would say there was something amiss between you and Jade. I saw the way she turned down the water. What's up with you two, Ed? Man to man, you can speak frankly to me."

Ed huffed a quiet laugh. "Ok, sir. Man to man, your daughter has me puzzled. We got in a tiff a couple of days ago and I am trying to smooth things over with her. I spoke with Rand about it and he advised that I show her kindness, no matter her reaction. I'm not used to the cold shoulder. When Jade and I first met....sure, I was attracted to her. She's pretty, funny, godly. I don't need to spell out her special qualities to you. You're her dad; you know them. Several of our conversations have revealed to me that Jade and I aren't 'on the same level,' as she calls it, in our relationship with Christ. So this *level* has created a barrier between our friendship and it's what we had words about the other day. We definitely don't see eye to eye on this. Jade believes she is up here," Ed paused and held his hand up above his head, "and I am down here." He then lowered his hand to waist-level indicating where he was in Jade's eyes. "Yet, I still want to be her friend. Maybe I am trying too hard. Maybe we just aren't meant to be friends."

"Wow. I am really sorry that my daughter has communicated to you that you two are on different *levels*. I hope you believe that neither her mother nor I have encouraged her to choose friends because of this viewpoint of hers. I've seen her treat people differently before, especially young men like yourself, and now I know why. Don't give up on a friendship with Jade. You have a lot to offer as a friend, Ed. And it sounds like Rand gave you some sound advice." John swallowed the last of his water and picked up his shovel again to resume working. He paused and looked Ed in the eyes. "You're a good man, Ed. I would consider it an honor if you ever were Jade's friend."

Ed smiled for the first time that day. *Who would have thought the father of the girl I was at odds with would have paid me such a high compliment?* Bemused, Ed picked up his rake feeling a bit lighter than before.

*********************

He saw them again. Gabe discreetly looked into the trees and knew he could see eyes watching the beginnings of the clean-up project. *Why are they hiding? More importantly, why aren't they helping their own village? These men are young and should be lending a hand. I am just going to find out.*

Gabe glanced back down at his work and formulated a plan. He walked over to Rand. "Dad, don't look back, but there are eyes in the trees again. I think you and I should get to the bottom of who they belong to and why they aren't helping their village. Are you with me?"

Rand looked at his son. "Yes, I am. This isn't the first time they have wanted to remain unseen. Let's just approach them in a non-threatening way and maybe they will talk to us." He turned in the direction of the young men and the two started slowly walking towards the trees. Immediately they could see three young men duck into the trees. When Gabe and Rand reached the tree line, Rand called out, "Hey, we could sure use some help over here on cleaning up these burned houses. Can you guys give us a hand?"

Peter, Andrew, and Markus stopped in their tracks. Peter spoke first, "You have plenty of men helping. You don't need us. We have our own work to do." He reached to his waist and withdrew a knife and began casually tossing it in the air, catching it by its yellowed, bone handle.

Rand recognized the handle as possibly made of an antler. He knew the young man was trying to threaten him and Gabriel. Rand spoke calmly to the boys. "Did any of your family's homes burn? Or were they spared from the fire?"

Rand saw one of the boys shift uneasily at this question. The boy said, "My family is fine. Our home was spared. All of our family's are fine. Do not worry about us."

Gabe spoke up. "Can you spare a day and come help us do some clean up? Your village could really use the man-power."

The fidgety boy said, "Maybe I can spare a few hours. We could help awhile." He started to move towards Rand and Gabe but immediately Peter's hand snaked out and gripped the boy's shoulder causing him to wince.

"No, we cannot help. Remember we have a job this afternoon and we need to leave now." He spoke through gritted teeth at the other two.

Fear flared in the boys' eyes and they turned and followed their leader back through the trees without another word. The leader looked back and returned his knife to his waist again, shooting a threatening glance towards Rand and Gabe.

"That was unsuccessful. Who do you think they are, Gabe? Two of them look very familiar to me but I can't place their names. I know I have seen them on past trips."

"I don't know, but it's pretty easy to tell who the leader of the pack is. Let's get back." Gabe couldn't get back fast enough to the safety of the group.

When Peter, Andrew, and Markus had gone far enough into the woods, Peter stopped and turned on the other two. "Do not speak to them ever again! You know how we feel about the Americans! They are here to change us, make us like them. They think we are stupid Indians and have no respect for us. We do not need them here. Now let's get the girls off this Island and go to Seal Harbor before they ask more questions." When the two boys didn't respond, Peter inched his face close to theirs and growled, "Do you hear me?"

Both Andrew and Markus nodded in unison and followed Peter down the path towards the hide-out and the waiting girls. Their fun for the weekend was over with the intrusion of the missionaries.

# CHAPTER 30

The next two days wore on for the team working side by side with their precious Aleutian friends. Relationships were forged and hearts knit together even more closely than before, something hard work and good fellowship seemed to promote. Gabe glanced around at all that had been accomplished these past two days. His team had worked tirelessly and now had all of the seven burned down homes removed and the rubble burned. They were now awaiting his return trip when he would go back to Fairbanks and bring more supplies to rebuild for these families.

Gabriel had spent the last two days engrossed in a couple of things. First, he was planning with the families what size home they needed to rebuild and the materials for the job. And he had spent many extra moments in Luka's home at the bedside of Rose.

Since her fall through the ice, Rose had been sleeping almost the entire 48 hours. Lukas's mother had helped care for Rose since Natalia was busy with Ivan after his turn for the worse, and when she knew Ivan was sleeping Natalia would come to Luka's home and sit with Rose while she slept. Gabe only sat with Rose when one of the other women was present.

He would sit for an hour at a time, reading from his big, black, leather-bound Bible and wait for Rose to wake up.

After he had rescued her from the icy waters and ran to the village with Rose, Luka heard his cries for help as he neared their houses. She directed him to her own house and room and quickly got her mother to come care for Rose. Knowing Natalia had Ivan to care for, she quickly set to work on warming up Rose and doing what she could for the girl. Luka sent word to Natalia of Rose's accident and that she was being cared for at her home. Natalia came quickly to check on her Rose and accepted the help of her friends.

Gabe expressed his deep concern for Rose to Luka the day she fell through the ice "Luka, why is she sleeping so much? I am concerned about her. This isn't normal for someone to sleep this long after an event like this." Concern furrowed his handsome brow.

Luka looked into Gabe's blue eyes. "Gabriel, Rose will be fine. She needs rest. With the fire and everything else, life has been very trying on the Island in the last few weeks. I believe she is suffering from exhaustion more than anything. She needs to rest. Her body will wake up fully when it has rested enough." Luka smoothed her best friend's dark hair away from her face.

Gabe closed the pages he had been reading and caught the concern in Luka's voice. Luka and Gabe had become fast friends. He enjoyed talking to Luka. She was a wealth of information about life on the Aleutian Islands. "I know the fire took a toll on everyone, but what else has been going on? What would cause a young girl to collapse from exhaustion like this?"

Luka unconsciously reached a hand up to touch the red line on her pretty face. She looked down at the sewing in her lap and shrugged her small shoulders. "Nothing for you to worry about, Gabe. All will work out in the end."

Gabe saw Luka's hand reach for the red line on her face. "Luka, tell me. Maybe we can help. That's why we are here, to help you and your people. You can trust me, Luka."

Tears formed in her eyes, but Luka quickly blinked them away. "Gabriel, we have suffered many things in the past few months. I am afraid to tell you. But at the same time, we need help. We at least need your prayers."

She hesitated for a moment then took a deep shuddering breath. "Rose's brother and my brother have been very foolish. They are a little older than Rose and I, both are twenty. You remember them, Andrew and Markus. They have a friend who is twenty-one and he is not a good influence on the boys. This friend," Luka paused and touched

207

her red cheek again, "is a bad person. He brings alcohol to our brothers and girls to the island; most of the girls are my age. They come here to spend the weekend with the boys and do things that I will not speak of. Usually for payment of money, sometimes for a hot meal and alcohol. The brothers are now stealing from our fathers and selling their stolen items in Seal Harbor on the mainland where the girls are from. I have heard many things in secret spoken between Markus and Andrew, and this friend, Peter. They have a hide-out away from the village where they secretly meet and bring the girls and drink their alcohol. Our parents are unaware of the stealing but are grieved by the alcohol and the absence of their sons. Gabriel, it is too much for this small island. The Council has chosen to stay out of it for many reasons. It will ruin us if they aren't stopped. The future generations will be greatly affected by this evil. I have secretly planned to go to the Alaska State Troopers for their help because the Council seems powerless or unwilling to do anything about this problem. My father will travel to Seal Harbor soon for fishing and trapping gear and I will go with him and then talk to the AST." She paused for a breath and buried her face in her hands.

Looking up quickly, she gasped, "Gabriel, I have told you so much more than I should have. Please honor me and my people and do not say a word! Swear to me you will not tell anyone of my plan. It could bring harm to me and my family if I am to blame for going to the authorities. Swear to me, Gabriel!" She grasped his arm tightly and looked pleadingly into Gabe's eyes.

Gabe laid a hand on Luka's shoulder. "Thank you, Luka, for telling me. I had no idea. Boot-legging and prostitution is very serious. Yes, we will pray. I would like your permission to discuss these things privately with my father and see what he says. We have seen at least three young men watching us on several occasion, but they obviously don't want to be seen. Do you think it is them?" Luka nodded in answer. Gabe pressed further, "Luka, what happened to your face?"

At his quiet question, Luka burst into tears. Gabe laid a hand on her shoulder. She looked up after a moment and said one word. "Peter."

Gabe shuddered at the thought of what Peter was capable of. Bringing alcohol to his minor friends, paying for young girls to come to the island for their own pleasure, hurting Luka. Something had to be done soon. Gabe vowed to talk to Rand that very day and do some research of his own into how these types of matters were handled on the Islands when he returned to Fairbanks. Until then, he could pray.

Startling him and Luka from their conversation, Rose reached up a slender hand and grasped the blue sleeve of Gabe's shirt, her eyes flying open. She looked around the room and then back at Gabe. Her eyes blinked several times then, in a quiet, awe-filled whisper, she said, "My rescuer! You are from my dream. You saved me!" Tears flooded her eyes as she clung to Gabe's sleeve even tighter.

Gabe and Luka exchanged confused glances. For two days Rose had been murmuring in her sleep. Oftentimes she would say Gabriel's name, sending heat flooding his cheeks. Luka would glance at him and shrug her shoulders. Then she would let out a pitiful scream and grasp the air trying to grab hold of something, anything. Luka and Gabe felt she was reliving the accident in those moments of terror. They would quickly calm Rose and she would drift off to sleep again.

This wide-eyed gaze and her quiet words gave them hope that she was now awake. Luka went to Rose's side. "Rose, everything's fine. You are safe and warm now. You are in my home, in my room. Do you remember the accident?"

Rose tore her gaze from Gabe's face. She licked parched lips and said just above a whisper, "Yes. The ice. It broke and I fell in the freezing waters. My arms and legs stung so badly. I choked on the water over and over. I remember someone yelling my name, then telling me to grab the limb. Then I saw blue arms wrap around me and felt someone lift me.....That's all I know." Rose took a deep breath. She looked back at Gabe. "You. You saved me. You were in my dream. You are my rescuer!" She glanced at Gabe's hands and spoke quietly, "The black book! From my dreams too."

He glanced down at his Bible he was holding. Confusion crossed his brow. Gabe had spent the last two days contemplating his own recurring dream from months past. He knew without a doubt that Rose was the one in his dream. He was destined to save her. God had given him the dream, the vivid dream-sounds and dream-pictures to be prepared to rescue Rose. It had shaken his world. Now Rose was talking about her own dream and he was in it! And his Bible, too? This all made no sense.

As quickly as she had awakened, Luka and Gabe watched her eyelids flutter and her quiet breathing resumed as she slept once again.

# CHAPTER 31

The missionary team had gathered for their last dinner together before leaving the Island for AMRA headquarters for a week. They enjoyed fresh fish, moose steaks, berries, and homemade bread. Yuri had supplied the meat and Lydia and her mother, Ola, had prepared it to perfection. They all enjoyed the restful evening before leaving tomorrow afternoon for the mainland. The evening bonfire blazed brightly while some of the team gathered around it after helping clean up after the meal.

Gabe was deep in conversation with Rand over Luka's news. Ed overheard bits and pieces and discreetly walked away from the two men to give them privacy. Jill and Becca were in Yuri's house visiting with the other women. Jade had just walked out with a steaming cup of tea in hand and settled herself by her dad and the fire. She glanced up at Ed as he came towards her.

John scooted over on the bench and made room for Ed on one end. "Are you ready to head back to the mainland and then Washington, Ed? I bet your baseball team back home will be ready to see you again."

"Yes and no, John. I do want to be there to finish out the school year, but I have really enjoyed my time here. I believe there's much more to be done on Datka than just rebuilding projects if you know what I mean. I think God just uses these projects as open doors for us to minister to the peoples' hearts, not just meet their physical needs. And I am looking forward to working this summer with you and your family some more."

John stood and patted Ed on the shoulder. "We've got a big summer ahead of us, that's for sure. Our work will definitely be cut out for us, but I can't think of a better team to work with than you and the Parkers. Good night, you two. I think I will turn in." John leaned down and kissed his silent daughter on the cheek then left to find Jill.

Ed glanced over at Jade. She was still cradling her tea in her hands. She gave him a quick side glance and remained silent. "Are you anxious to head back to the mainland, Jade? You have really worked yourself in the ground the last couple of weeks. I am really proud of you, the way you work as hard as anyone, and how you interact with the other women and children. You are a real asset to the team."

Jade was glad for the cover of dark as she felt her cheeks flush at Ed's comments. *Why am I blushing at Ed's words? That's silly, Jade. Get a grip on yourself,* she internally chided. Instead she spoke quietly to Ed, "Thanks. But I don't work any harder than the rest of our team. I guess I'll turn in, too. It's getting late."

*Well, I guess short and sweet is better than nothing, if you can call that sweet.* Ed shook his head and snorted to himself. *Rand doesn't have a clue what I am dealing with.* He watched Jade walk off wondering if the couple of months' separation would do their relationship more good than anything.

*********************

Jade was lying in her make-shift fur bed and tossing and turning. For the life of her, she couldn't get her mind to stop thinking. She now knew nothing more than friendship was going to occur between she and Gabe. She had seen the looks between him and Rose and knew of his vigilant wait at her bedside. Jade refused to allow jealousy to creep in over Rose and Gabe's friendship. She knew better than that. She also knew that her heart and time were better spent on someone who *wanted* to be her friend, someone who she didn't have to fight to get him to cast her a second glance. Gabe's interests were elsewhere and she had decided to respect that. Because of Gabe, she did know what type of man she wanted. Someone much like him.

As if on cue, her next thought was, *And not someone like Ed.* Instantly, her conscious prickled. Jade knew this was being unkind to Ed, which he had done nothing to deserve from her. So what if they didn't see eye to eye on some things. Did he deserve her constant cold shoulder? Jade knew she was attracted to Ed physically and to his personality. He was very charming and funny. She seemed to be the only person that didn't want to be around him. The haunting, unanswered questions returned for the hundredth time. *Why don't I want to be around Ed? Do I have a valid point about being on a different level than him? Or was Ed right when we argued the other day?*

His words played over again in her mind. *"We are different, but not like you think. You see, I've learned something lately. Even though I may have a very ugly, dirty, messed up past and made many wrong choices, I am no more a sinner than you are. Don't you see? It's not about upbringing or past actions or how holy a person lives. It's the heart of a person, Jade. And right now, your heart looks a lot like my past life!........Your pride and self-righteousness are as bad as all my years of drunkenness and wrong choices."*

His words made her cheeks flush again, but this time, not with anger as they originally had. Tonight, lying under her fur covers, she saw what she must really look like to Ed in all of her pride and self-righteousness. It wasn't a pretty sight. Ed had been nothing but kind to her after their argument on the shore. Jade knew she didn't deserve his friendship. She thought about how she had rejected his kindness and it made her face flame hotter with embarrassment. She felt the tears course down her cheeks. Jade let them flow for once. Cleansing tears, tears that needed to be shed because of the dirtiness of her heart, her arrogant attitude. How could she ever think she was *better than someone* because she read her Bible more, or had been raised in church or had wonderful, God-fearing parents or had lived a purer life?

Jade did what she needed to do long ago. She prayed. *Father God, please forgive me. I have been so foolish. I have not been a good example of You or Your Son, Jesus. I ask for You to forgive me for my attitude and haughtiness. Wash me clean from my sin. And God, if there is any way to make things right with Ed before he leaves tomorrow for the next two months, please show me how and give me the words. In Your Son's Name, Amen.*

Sighing deeply, she reached for her cross necklace. Jade fell into a peaceful sleep for the first time in many nights.

# CHAPTER 32

Eyelids heavy with the sleep of many hours, Rose slowly stretched her stiff body. It took a moment to realize she was in her best friend's room and bed. Slowly the last couple of days played across her mind. Gabriel saving her, sitting by her bed, her friend caring for her, the missionaries, the fire, her brother and his foolish friends......So much had happened; so much still had to take place.

Rose lifted her head and looked at her sleeping friend lying on a pallet of blankets near her. Muscles stiff with lack of use, Rose stretched again. *This must be what a bear feels like after hibernating,* she thought.

Reality washed over Rose as the rising sun washed over the Alaskan sky. *Oh, God! Thank You for saving me! I should be dead.* Then visions of her dying father flashed before her. Rose sat up quickly and felt every protesting muscle. She began gathering her clothes that were neatly folded in a pile near her bed and dressed silently.

Luka stirred close by. "Rose? You are awake!" Luka jumped up from her pallet and threw herself at Rose almost knocking them both down. The girls giggled and hugged tightly. "I was so worried about you, Rose. Someone else with blue eyes was too." Again girlish giggles filled the room.

Blushing deeply, Rose said, "Luka, I don't know what you are talking about. Now hush." She playfully gave her friend a little shove. Rose's expression turned very serious, a frown marking her pale forehead. "My father. Luka, what have you heard about him? I must go to him now."

"He was sleeping soundly last night. All is well, Rose. My mother came in very early this morning from your house and told me he was still alive. I fell asleep again until you awoke. But she fears he doesn't have long, Rose." Luka laid a comforting hand on her friend's arm.

Tears sprang to Rose's gold-flecked, green eyes. She covered her face with shaky hands. "I must find Andrew! Father wanted to speak to him. Before I ran off and fell in the ice, those were his last words to me. I have to get Andrew."

"Finish dressing and I will bring you something to eat before you leave. I haven't seen Markus or Andrew in several days. They have been around only for a few moments at a time and then quickly leave again. Markus hardly speaks to anyone. I will help you look for our brothers." Luka left Rose putting on her fur-trimmed boots and returned with dark brown bread and water for them to share.

The girls ate hastily and made plans to go separate ways looking for the boys. Hopefully they would find one or both of them soon. Luka wrapped an arm around Rose's shoulders and began to pray. "God of Creation, please help us find the boys quickly this morning. Please protect us. In Your Son's name, Amen."

The two headed in separate directions. Luka started for the shore and the fishing boats and Rose took off towards her parents' home. She had to see if Andrew had been home yet.

Rose neared her home and slowed down her pace. She was both afraid and anxious to go inside, afraid of the state she would find her father in, anxious to learn any news of his condition. She eased the door open and heard loud snoring. Andrew. Creeping to his side she bent over her snoring brother. Instantly she jerked her head back as the scent of alcohol reached her nostrils. She wanted to reach down and choke him! Instead, Rose nudged him roughly and whispered near his ear. "Andrew! Wake up! I must talk to you!"

Andrew rolled to his back and blinked heavy eyes at his sister. Cursing under his breath, he said, "Leave me alone. I am sleeping."

Overcome with a fierce anger and frustration with Andrew, Rose grabbed him by his dirty shirt front and shook Andrew a few times. Her teeth clenched, she whispered, "Now, Andrew!"

Andrew frowned and sat up. "What is wrong with you, Rose? Give me a minute to wake up." He shoved her hand away.

Rose wasn't going to be deterred any longer. She grabbed his arm and half-drug Andrew to a standing position, surprised at her own strength. "We are going outside now. So get up on your own or I will drag you out the door."

Andrew stumbled to his feet while his little sister shoved him out the front door. Pent up questions poured from her as she faced her brother who was struggling to open his eyes against the early morning light. "Andrew, you look horrible. Where have you been? Do you know what condition our father is in, or do you even care anymore? Why did you come home? Did you run out of money and come to steal again?" Rose had never before spoken so boldly to Andrew before, especially since his foolish ways.

Shame filled her brother's face. He looked at the ground, then back at Rose. "You do not know what you are talking about. I do not need father or his money. Nor have I stolen anything that is not rightfully mine. I came home for-for more clothes," he stammered. "What about father's condition? He was sleeping when I got home last night. So was mother. I just need to get my things and leave. I have work to do on the mainland." He started to walk away from Rose, but she wasn't going to be brushed off again.

Grabbing his arm, Rose jerked Andrew back to face her. With her voice low, she spoke words that needed to be said. "You have no idea the trouble you and your friends are causing here on the Island. And you do not care. I do not know you, Andrew. What has happened? You think your friends and your girls and your alcohol are a big secret? It is not! You are destroying yourself and our family. I have seen you take from father both money and fishing gear. And now he is lying in his bed dying while you run off again. All he wants is to see you before he leaves this earth. You owe him that much," she hissed inches from her brother's surprised face.

Emotions flashed across Andrew's face while she spoke, anger, fear, guilt, shame, and lastly, a cold, hard, indifference. "You are a foolish girl, Rose, and will do well to stay away from me and my friends. I will go see father one last time and then I am leaving this horrible place." He spat on the ground and jerked away from her grip.

Tears sprang to Rose's eyes as she watched her stranger-brother stalk away. Rose followed close behind and entered the house on his heels.

Natalia was in the kitchen preparing Ivan's morning medicine. She looked up from her task. "Andrew! You are home! Rose! My dear girl! Why are you out of bed? Are you better? Oh, I have been so worried about both of my children." Tears poured down Natalia's face as she fell into Rose's arms.

Andrew headed straight to his room. Rose calmed and quieted her mother. She looked into Natalia's eyes and spoke quietly. "Andrew is only home to get some of his things and to see father. I am doing very well. I just needed to rest, but I am fine, just a little stiff. How is father?"

Natalia sighed deeply. "Not well, Rose. I am surprised he lived through the night. His breathing is very raspy this morning. I came for his medicine when you two arrived. Ivan doesn't know of your accident. He has slept most of the days and nights since you fell. He will be so glad to see you. And Andrew."

Rose followed her mother into their bedroom and immediately heard her father's breathing. It terrified Rose. She had never heard him so raspy before. "Mother, this is bad. What can we do for him?" Rose knelt by her father's side and took his hand in hers.

"Father, it's me. Rose. How are you?" He stirred at her voice. It took a moment for him to open his eyes, but hearing Rose's voice seemed to give him momentary strength.

In a whispered voice, Ivan said, "Rose, my girl." Ivan just smiled at Rose a moment taking in her beauty. "I will miss you when I am gone. Please sing for me again."

Barely able to breathe, Rose tried her best to calm her raging emotions. She could not imagine her life without her father. Seeing his struggle to draw air and live was enough to crush her chest with a weight so heavy she thought she might die with him. Wanting to please her father more than anything in the world at that moment, Rose sang with tear-filled words a song that Ivan's own mother had taught her.

*"Love so sweet*
*Hearts so dear*
*Nothing can separate*
*Two souls entwined.*

*Near or far*
*Timeless love*
*Hearts entwined*
*Evermore"*

Ivan sighed and looked at her again. "Thank you, Rose. Please tell me. Is Andrew coming? I want to see him."

Rose stood. "Yes, father. Let me get him."

Leaving his side was the hardest thing Rose had ever done. She knew her father would be gone soon. She went to Andrew and spoke quickly, "Father wants to see you. Come quickly."

Andrew entered the room, not knowing what to expect. It had been months since he last saw his once strong father. Now he was lying on his bed, frail and pitiful under a blanket. His hair was longer than usual and his face very pale. What struck Andrew the most was Ivan's raspy, rattling breaths. It caused unbidden tears to spring to Andrew's eyes, which he quickly choked down. Purposing to keep his focus, Andrew let visions of Berta and his friends and the bottles full of amber liquid float before his blurry eyes instead. He had come home to get more of his belongings and to see if there was any more money hidden somewhere, not to watch his father die. Andrew stood by Ivan's bedside, unable to kneel and embrace his father. Guilt and shame had created a chasm so deep and wide that prevented him from reaching out to his dying father.

Ivan looked at Natalia and Rose. "Please leave us alone a moment." The two women left so father and son could speak in private.

Ivan reached a frail hand up to his unresponsive son and slowly let it drop to his side again. Breathing deeply so he could speak, Ivan looked at Andrew. "Son, I am leaving soon. You must stay and care for your mother and sister when I am gone. I need you to do this for me. To be the man, provider, protector of these two precious souls." Ivan stopped and coughed. Blood covered the cloth he used to cover his mouth with. Oblivious to it, he pressed on. "Do you understand me, Andrew? I need you now more than ever. It is up to you."

Anger flashed across Andrew's face. His nostrils flared with unspoken words. He placed his hands on his hips and glared at his father. "You will be fine, father. Rest and medicine will do you good. I cannot care for these two! I am one man, with a life of my own to live. When you recover fully you can care for them again. I have work on the mainland waiting for me and can't stay around here much longer."

Hurt filled Ivan's eyes. He whispered, "As I suspected." Ivan closed his eyes once more for a moment. "Andrew, you are needed here. I am a dying man who cannot take care of these two any longer. Stay and do what is your duty for your family."

"That is what you have always wanted and expected from me, father, to do my *duty*. This is not *my* duty, but *yours*. I must find my own life and it won't be here on Datka! There are others on the Island to help mother and Rose. You will get well soon and resume your duty. I will return in a few weeks and see you again, but I will *not* stay here forever."

"You would *deny* your family and their needs for your friends and your own life?" Momentary strength and anger at his son's words pushed Ivan to his elbows to challenge him one last time.

When Andrew said nothing, Ivan clearly knew the answer. He looked into his son's eyes and spoke firmly but quietly. "Then leave now and do not return. I love you no matter your actions, but you must leave *now!* You are no longer welcome here." Ivan fell back onto the pillow and closed his eyes, tears seeping from their corners.

Teeth gritted, Andrew spoke to Ivan. "You do not have to ask me twice. Consider me gone forever." He left the house without a backwards glance nor did he take his things with him.

As soon as Natalia and Rose saw Andrew leave the house, they rushed to Ivan's side. Again he was having a coughing fit, which produced even more blood. Natalia reached for a clean cloth for him. Both women were crying silently as they watched his suffering. "Ivan, where did you send Andrew? He left just now."

His one-word answer startled them both. "Away."

"Father, what do you mean 'away?' Andrew is needed here, especially now. He must work for us and help us since you are so sick. When will he return?" Rose panicked.

"Listen to me, girls. I sent Andrew away from here. I know everything he has been doing and will not have it defile you. His choices are not good." Ivan closed weary eyes again.

Natalia gently shook his shoulder. "Ivan, we *need* Andrew! He cannot leave!"

Rose spoke next. "Father, you cannot send him away. This is not wise. He should be made to stay home. He has to take your place as the head of this family."

Both women thought he was sleeping again. For several minutes Ivan didn't speak. He opened teary eyes and spoke to them. "Rose, remember when you were little and we were walking one day and came upon the mother bear and her cub? The cub kept venturing too close to the rocky ledge and would not heed his mother's pushing him back. She finally swatted him so hard with her massive paw that he yelped in pain and his hip was bleeding from her claws. But it stopped him from going over the edge right then."

He paused for a deep breath. "Some time later we saw this same mother and cub and she was trying to get him to follow her, but he kept getting distracted by all of his surroundings. Rose, remember you cried as we watched her leave her cub after roaring repeatedly for him and he just ignored her. She went her own way and let him run off on his own. She *knew* her cub would no longer follow her. The mother bear had to let him go his own way. I had to let your brother go his own way. Only I sent him off, not to return and bring harm here any longer. You must understand. It grieves my heart more than anything. I am an old man and wanted to see my son choose his family and what is right. But he didn't. My heart is broken now." Tears coursed down his face.

All three of them cried tears of remorse and regret knowing Ivan had done the right thing in telling Andrew to leave and letting him go his own way.

Taking a deep, shuddering, last breath, Ivan looked again into his beloved girls' faces. "My hope is we will see each other soon. My heart is comforted knowing that God will care for you in my absence. That is why I can leave at peace. You are in God's strong, mighty hands, dear girls."

With those final words, a beautiful, peaceful smile spread across Ivan's face as he held each of his girls' hands.

********************

As Luka neared the shore, she heard voices and laughter. She immediately recognized who was ahead. Ducking behind the sedges, Luka could still see the shore before her. Luka watched as the group of young people was loading their things on a small boat. She could discern snatches of their conversations.

"…..leave now we will reach Seal Harbor before the storm hits……"

"…..hurry and get you girls back…..do not want the missionaries to find out….."

She watched from her hidden spot as they boarded the boats. Once again the missionaries had brought relief to the Island, although they were unaware of this. Today evil was leaving because of the missionaries' presence, and Luka was just as determined to do something permanent about it as soon         as         her         chance         arose.

# CHAPTER 33

*April, 1968*

While the team finished up breakfast nearing their final days before flying to Fairbanks, Gabe looked up to see a wonderful surprise. Rose was walking straight towards him, cheeks red and her gait strong. She had on a light-weight fur parka and simple boots. Rose had never looked more beautiful and alive to him.

Rose had her eyes set on Gabriel. She had some things to say to him, things that might burn a hole in her heart if left unsaid. "Gabriel, can we go for a walk? I need to talk to you," she said in her sweet, quiet way. The urgency of this walk was written all over her face.

Smiling bigger than he had in days, Gabe said, "Sure, Rose. Let me tell the others I will be gone for a bit." He left her standing, twisting the edge of her parka between her fingers.

Gabe quickly returned to her side. "Which way? I will follow you, Rose." She started walking while he continued to speak, "You look wonderful, Rose! I am so glad to see you up and around. I was worried about you." He paused at her slight flush. After seeing her back to her old self again and not lying in bed as she had been for those long days, Gabe took note of the faster beat of his heart.

"Thank you, Gabriel. It is good to be awake and out of bed. I feel like a bear just waking from hibernation." She giggled and looked down self-consciously. "Let's walk to my favorite spot. I have missed going there."

She gave a whistle and almost instantly Stormy was at her side. Rose placed a hand on the dog's head while she walked. "Oh, I have missed my Stormy, too. She is my constant companion. I was surprised to see your face when I awakened the other day instead of Stormy's." Again Rose giggled.

Gabe loved to hear the sound of her laughter. He didn't realize how much he had missed it until she was sleeping quietly for those few days. Rose had been such a part of his days leading up to the accident that he was surprised at how much he had missed her quiet presence. She was able to fill in so many gaps while he communicated with the Aleutians and helped him get reacquainted with Island life. Her quiet, unassuming presence brought him much joy and peace. "So where are we going, Rose?"

"To a special spot on the shore. My grandfather used to bring me here when I was a child. The day is beautiful to sit and talk a minute. That is if you don't mind." She blushed deeply as she realized how presumptuous she had been asking him to walk with her. "I know you are busy so I won't keep you away for long. It is just right around this bend." Rose stumbled on a rock protruding from the ground and almost fell.

Gabe instantly reached out and caught her around the waist and easily kept her from falling down. He held on until she had her footing once again.

"You must stop doing that, you know. You cannot keep rescuing me, Gabriel. This is the second time you have been my rescuer." Her laughter reached his ears as he realized she was teasing him.

"Well, then you must stop falling so much!" Gabe's heart lurched at her words. He knew he wasn't her rescuer, but God was. This was the second time she had referred to him as such and it bothered him that she saw him in such a way. "Rose, let's sit here on this rock and rest a minute. Your legs aren't as strong as you think after being in bed for so long." Placing a strong hand on her back, he guided her to the boulder on their left.

"Good choice, Gabriel. This is the spot I was leading you to. My favorite boulder. Look around us. What do you see?" She inhaled deeply from the coastal air. The birds were soaring over the water in search of lunch. The sun was a brilliant, blazing ball overhead adding its own touch to the day.

Gabe breathed deeply too. He looked around and understood why this was a favorite spot. They had walked up a gradual incline and now sat on a boulder that overlooked the water and shoreline not fifteen feet below them. The sky was gorgeous, not a trace of fog or clouds which was unusual for the Island. "You can see for miles, water straight ahead of us and sky all above. This is beautiful, Rose. I see why you love it here. The contrast of blues and greens is breathtaking."

"See that spot on the shoreline below us? My grandfather brought me here as a little girl and taught me to skip rocks and look for beautiful shells and rocks for my collection. He taught me many things on that very spot." Her eyes took on a faraway gaze.

"What is something he taught you? What are you remembering about him right now?" Gabe admired her profile, again his heart quickening its pace.

Surprised that he could so easily guess the direction of her thoughts, she said, "I will tell you the most important lesson he ever taught me. It is about how our lives are like a stone tossed into the water. The ripples that one stone creates goes on and on, just like the ripple-affect we can have on people." She then gave him a detailed account of her precious grandfather's unforgettable words.

After Rose finished recounting the story of her grandfather, Gabe leaned back on his hands and pondered the words. "That is wonderful, Rose. Very wise and true words. Thank you for telling me that. It will shape how I live my life, knowing all of my actions count and affect others."

A moment later, Gabe looked over at Rose, "I know that's not why you asked me to come talk with you. What is on your mind?" He nudged her playfully on her shoulder with his own.

Gathering her courage, Rose looked directly at Gabe, "I know that I owe you my life, but have no way to repay you for saving me, Gabriel. I have been taught by my ancestors to never let a debt go unpaid. But how do I pay back a debt such as this?" Rose rushed on. "I dreamed of you and your black book. Many times. It even scared me some nights because I had the same dream over and over. I know it was you in my dream. You are my rescuer and I must repay, but how? My life cannot be forever indebted to you. Tell me what to do, how to repay you."

Gabe took her by the shoulders when he saw how distressed she had become. "Rose, stop. Listen to me. You don't owe me anything. I did not save or rescue you."

Confusion shone in her beautiful green-brown eyes. "You did not save me? Yes, Gabriel, it was you. I know it was."

Out of determination to get Rose to see the truth, Gabe's response was a bit too harsh as he tried to get her to listen. "No, Rose! I can save no one! God did it. He rescued you, not me. I was just His tool to get you out of the water. Rose, I had dreams too. Dreams of a girl screaming and falling and reaching out to me. Over and over, I would have this dream. It haunted me because I couldn't save the girl; I couldn't reach her hands. I couldn't even see her face. Don't you see? God gave me the dreams so I would be prepared to save you. I didn't understand them when I would have them but when you were lying in bed recovering, I understood completely what had happened. Don't you see?" Pausing, Gabe let her take his words in. He continued, "Rose, it sounds like God gave you dreams, too. Tell me your dreams."

Rose took a deep breath to gather her jumbled thoughts. She gave him a detailed picture of her dreams of a man in blue, with eyes bluer than the sky above them. Of strong hands reaching out to her with colorful toys and a large black book that scared her in her dreams because she didn't know what it said. She was both attracted to and scared of the book. "Gabriel, I do not understand what you mean by you did not rescue me. *You* pulled me out of the waters and kept me from drowning. *You* carried me and kept me from dying. It *was* you."

Suddenly Gabe understood Rose's dream and the black book. His face light up with a smile. He stood from the rock and removed a small black book from his jacket pocket.

"That's like the book in my dreams, only much smaller. What is it, Gabriel? Tell me." Her eyes grew large and she sat stone-still waiting for him to read something full of doom or some sentence of judgment over her, wondering what awful things the black book foretold.

"Oh, Rose, this book is *life,* not anything scary. It is my Bible, a smaller version of the larger one I was reading in your room." He couldn't contain his excitement at this point.

Rose interrupted him a moment. "I remember now the larger one. I saw you holding it when I was in bed at Luka's house. It is the same?"

"Yes, Rose. Only smaller. The words are the exact same, words of life. Listen to this, God's very words written to all of mankind, even to you, Rose. *'When you pass through the waters, I will be with you; and when you pass through the rivers, they will not sweep over you. When you walk through the fire, you will not be burned; the flames will not set you ablaze.'"* Gabe looked up into her tear-filled eyes.

"That was written for me? To me?" Rose asked. She wiped at the tears running down her cheeks.

"Yes, Rose, for you. God's promise to you. *He* rescued you. *He* is your rescuer! Do you see?" Gabe prayed quietly for her to see the truth of these words.

She laughed and then choked out, "Yes! I do see! You are right, Gabriel. I have heard Bible stories from the missionaries before but thought of them as tales about other peoples' lives. I have never read the Bible as written to me. God is my Rescuer! He did save me from the water and fire. I did not drown or get burned." Her awe-filled eyes let him know she understood.

Instinctively, Rose stood and hugged Gabe and laughed again. Realizing what she had just done, she quickly pulled away and said, "We better return before they come looking for us."

Hope surged through Gabe and joy unspeakable. Another precious soul had just learned of God's saving love and grace. *This* is what his life was to be about.

# CHAPTER 34

After a quick early morning breakfast, the team began packing their bags and preparing for the flight to Fairbanks for the week. With lists ready of what to bring back and promises made to their Aleutian friends that they would soon return, the team walked towards their waiting planes that were now sitting like two lone birds on the shore. John, Gabe, and Rand began loading bags and luggage while the women hugged their friends and gave last minute farewells. Rand, Becca, and Ed would take one plane and fly to Juneau's airport for their return flight to Washington to finish up the school year. The Millers and Gabe would board the other plane for Fairbanks.

John glanced around for Jade and saw her about twenty yards away. Her back was to him and he could see Ed standing in front of her with his head down listening to what she had to say.

Jade had purposefully lagged behind the group walking to the waiting plane. She had seen Ed go back to Isaac, or "Little Bear" as Ed had nick-named him. Isaac's sad face stopped Ed in his tracks. He reached into his bag and retrieved a bright, small, toy top and bent down to Little Bear's level. Ed was on his knees in front of the little boy showing him how to make the top spin. Little Bear's face lit up with a smile brighter than the noonday sun. Ed promised him that he would return soon with even more surprises. He hugged the little boy and stood to leave.

Jade walked in front of Ed. He tried to side-step her and said a quick, "Excuse me, Jade."

Reaching out a hand, Jade stopped Ed. "Wait, please, Ed. I want to talk to you before we leave."

Ed stopped and raised his eyebrows. "Yeah, Little Lady?"

Jade looked down at her feet and shifted her stance. She shot a quick glance up at Ed's serious face and struggled to get her nerve up to say the words she needed to say. Taking a deep breath she spoke, "I know we are both about to board two separate planes and be separated for a couple of months. I don't blame you if you are happy about that. Ed, I have been just horrible to you. I am really sorry for being so judgmental and unkind. I don't want us to go our separate ways not being friends and leaving things unsaid. I know you were right when we argued on the shore. I have been wrong in my view of people and how God sees us. Please, will you forgive me?"

Ed shuffled his feet and was quiet for a moment. He glanced toward Rand who stood off by the planes looking in his direction. *I guess Rand knew what he was talking about after all.* Then his half-grin spread over his tanned face. "I wasn't exactly gentlemanly towards you, Jade. Yes, I forgive you. Please don't get mad when I say this. As a friend, I will miss you when I am in Washington." Ed held up his hands in defense. "I'm not implying anything more than that so don't get your feathers ruffled, Little Lady."

Jade felt her face flush and she quickly looked down. As she did, she reached up and unfastened the leather cord from behind her neck. "Well, Tex, this little lady is going to miss you too. Can I leave you my cross to wear while we are apart, maybe as a symbol of our truce and new friendship?" She shyly reached up and fastened her jade cross around Ed's neck as she spoke.

He looked into her eyes and reached up to finger the beautiful cross. "I would be honored to wear it, Jade."

With that, the two picked up their bags and headed to the awaiting planes. Not another word was spoken between them before they departed. Jade gave Ed a final little wave and got on the plane with her parents and Gabe. She smiled to herself as she noticed Ed's left hand grasping the jade cross as he climbed aboard to go his separate way. Maybe he had forgiven her after all.

********************

Gabe's heart was torn. He saw Rose standing apart from the group as they were boarding the plane. She looked sad. Gabe spoke to Rand before boarding the plane. "Dad, I need to take care of something. I'll be right back."

"Okay, Son. We still have about fifteen minutes before the pilot wants to leave. Take your time." Rand watched Gabe walk towards the lone girl, Rose. Her smile lit her pretty face when she saw Gabe walking towards her.

"Rose, I came to say good-bye. You know we will be back in a week with more supplies. Since there will be a whole lot less for you to do during the next week until our return, I want you to try to do something for me." He looked her directly in her green eyes.

"I will try, Gabriel. What is it?" She looked tentatively in his handsome face.

Never was Gabe more grateful that the Aleutian children were taught to read and write English at an early age. He reached into his jacket pocket and withdrew the small, black Bible. "When you have some free time, read where I have placed this ribbon. It's the book of John. It will tell you about Jesus and His great love for the world, for you, Rose. Then we will talk when I return. What do you think?"

Rose reached long, slender fingers for the book. "Yes, I will read it. Thank you."

"One more thing, Rose." He reached into his jeans pocket and withdrew something small and pink. "I found this on my morning walk today. It made me think of you. I want you to know that you have had a ripple-affect on my life." He took her hand in his and placed a small, pink heart-shaped rock in her palm. "Remember, your life has touched mine. Good-bye, Rose."

She looked at the tiny rock. Tears glimmered in her eyes, but her smile shone brightly. "And yours has touched mine. Thank you. Good-bye, Gabriel."

He turned and walked to the small plane. After he boarded the small craft and sat in his seat, Gabriel looked out the opposite window and watched a black-haired girl and her father rowing a small boat towards Seal Harbor. Gabe glanced at Rand and saw he was looking at the same thing. Quietly he uttered a heart-felt prayer. *Dear God, please guide and protect Luka and give her the wisdom she needs.*

Gabe leaned back in his plane seat ready to head to Fairbanks. He knew that the sooner he got there and began the week's work, the sooner he could return to Datka Island and the girl holding the heart-shaped rock.

LOOK FOR BOOK 2

OF

*ALASKA'S ALEUTIAN ISLANDS SERIES*

## RETURNED

**COMING WINTER 2013**

# ABOUT THE AUTHOR

Trudy Samsill is a resident of Paradise, Texas. She is wife to her best friend and soul-mate of 26 years and mother to 3 wonderful sons and 1 sweet princess. Trudy has been a home-school mom for 20 years, having graduated 2 sons and continuing to homeschool the last two, a sophomore and 5th grader. She recently graduated from Louisiana Baptist University with her Associates of Arts in Elementary Education in the Spring of 2013. Her first passion is writing, desiring her written words to touch her readers, to bring hope and inspiration towards greatness. She has a great love for nature, especially birds and wildflowers that flourish on their 11 acre homestead. Trudy is passionate about her relationship with God, above all else, giving Him all glory for this gift of words entrusted to her.

Trudy can also be found on her blog at trusoulshade.blogspot.com.

Please check out her first e-book venture, a short story, <u>Glass Marbles</u>. Here is the link to this book sold on Amazon: http://www.amazon.com/Glass-Marbles-ebook/dp/B00ASFMKO6/ref=sr_1_1?s=books&ie=UTF8&qid=1377523047&sr=1-1&keywords=glass+marbles

Made in the USA
Middletown, DE
22 December 2023

46640369R00141